Omens, taboos, prophecies: it's all part of everyday life for the Gypsies. The traditional Gypsy uses herbal lore, basic magic, and divination for practical matters. Knowledge of herbs is essential for Gypsy-style healing. Gypsy spells and charms favorably influence events. Using "the Sight" leads to making better choices and clearer decisions.

All of these practices are used by the shuvani, the Gypsy witch or shaman. The shuvani is the keeper of a tribe's magic, rites, and superstitions. Shuvanis can bless, curse, or heal as they see fit. Their powers, like those of the old Pagan peoples, are rooted in a belief in spirits of the earth, water, air, forest, and fields.

Gypsy Witchcraft & Magic reveals many working secrets of the shuvanis. Use this book as your reference source. Dip into it here and there for your enlightenment—or study the details of using knot magic, hair charms, herbal cures, or other old-world magical techniques. Discover the "hedge wisdom" of the shuvanis when you invite the time-honored magic of the Gypsies into your life.

About the Author

Ray Buckland's grandfather was the first of the Buckland Gypsies to give up traveling the roads in a wagon and to settle in a permanent house. From his earliest years, Ray remembers listening to his father's and grandfather's tales of Romani life, and watching his grandmother read cards and tell fortunes. At an early age, Ray Buckland started his own serious study of the Old Knowledge and later came to write about it in a number of best-selling books. "Buckland" is a well-known name among English Gypsies, and Ray Buckland has become a well-known author of books on practical magic.

To Write to the Author

If you wish to contact the author or would like more information about this book, please write to the author in care of Llewellyn Worldwide, and we will forward your request. Both the author and publisher appreciate hearing from you and learning of your enjoyment of this book and how it has helped you. Llewellyn Worldwide cannot guarantee that every letter written to the author can be answered, but all will be forwarded. Please write to:

Llewellyn Worldwide Ltd.
P.O. Box 64383, Dept. K097–3
St. Paul, MN 55164-0383, U.S.A.

Please enclose a self-addressed, stamped envelope for reply or $1.00 to cover costs. If outside the U.S.A., enclose international postal reply coupon.

Gypsy
Witchcraft & Magic

RAYMOND BUCKLAND

ILLUSTRATED BY MICHELLE DILLAIRE

1998
Llewellyn Publications
St. Paul, Minnesota 55164-0383, U.S.A.

FIRST EDITION
Second Printing, 1998

Cover design by Lisa Novak
Cover photo from University of Liverpool Photo Archives
Photo section images by courtesy of The University of Liverpool Library
    Reference (in order as printed): SM 1.22; SM/DY 5.3; SM/F 4.2; SM/F 7.20; SM/F.31; SM/DY 4.21; SM/DY 3.10; SM/DY 5.10; SM/C .57; SM/E .51; SM/DY 1.19; SMCG F-I.30; SM .43; Gal15.jpg; SM/F 5.6; SMCG/F 7.3
Interior photos by Raymond Buckland and Doug Deutscher
Interior art by Michelle Dillaire
Editing and interior design by Connie Hill

Library of Congress Cataloging-in-Publication Data
Buckland, Raymond, 1934–
    Gypsy witchcraft & magic / Raymond Buckland : illustrated by Michelle Dillaire. — 1st ed.
        p.   cm.
    Includes bibliographical references and index.
    ISBN 1–56718–097–3 (trade paper)
    1. Witchcraft.   2. Gypsies.   I. Title.
BF1566.B765   1998
133.4'3'0891497—dc21   98–22354
                                                                                    CIP

Llewellyn Worldwide does not participate in, endorse, or have any authority or responsibility concerning private business transactions between our authors and the public.

All mail addressed to the author is forwarded but the publisher cannot, unless specifically instructed by the author, give out an address or phone number.

Llewellyn Publications
A Division of Llewellyn Worldwide, Ltd.
P.O. Box 64383, Dept. K097–3
St. Paul, Minnesota 55164-0383, U.S.A.

Printed in the U.S.A.

Parika tut 'te sor kushtipen fon puv. Ajaw.
(Thank you for all goodness from the earth. Amen.)

For Tara, *mandi's jivaben ta mandi's komipen,*
and for Peter Ingram, *mandi's pral.*

OTHER BOOKS BY THE AUTHOR

Published by Llewellyn Worldwide, Ltd.

Practical Candleburning Rituals (1970, 1976, 1982)

Witchcraft from the Inside (1971, 1975, 1995)

Practical Color Magick (1983)

Buckland's Complete Book of Witchcraft (1986)

Secrets of Gypsy Fortunetelling (1988)

Secrets of Gypsy Dream Reading (1990)

Secrets of Gypsy Love Magic (1990)

Scottish Witchcraft (1991)

Doors to Other Worlds (1993)

The Committee (Fiction, 1993)

Truth About Spirit Communication (1995)

The Buckland Gypsies' Domino Divination Deck (1995)

Advanced Candle Magick (1996)

Cardinal's Sin (Fiction, 1996)

Gypsy Fortune Telling Tarot Kit (Book and Deck, 1998)

With Other Publishers

Witchcraft...the Religion (Buckland Museum, 1966)

A Pocket Guide to the Supernatural (Ace, 1969)

Witchcraft Ancient and Modern (HC, 1970)

Mu Revealed (Warner Paperback Library, 1970)
    under the pseudonym "Tony Earll"

Here is the Occult (HC, 1974)

The Tree: Complete Book of Saxon Witchcraft (Weiser, 1974)

Amazing Secrets of the Psychic World (Parker, 1975)
    with Hereward Carrington

Anatomy of the Occult (Weiser, 1977)

The Magic of Chant-o-Matics (Parker, 1978)

The Book of African Divination (Inner Traditions, 1992)
    with Kathleen Binger

Ray Buckland's Magic Cauldron (Galde Press, 1995)

Contents

꧁꧂

Preface

The pendulum swings, in all things. In the folklore of the Romany—the Gypsies—the pendulum has swung from the romanticism of the nineteenth century to the harsh reality of the late twentieth century. In recent books, the trend had been to focus on Gypsies in their near-poverty, their cramped quarters, and their frequently unhygienic environment. Emphasis today seems to be on the "lot" of the Gypsy, as an outcast desperately needing to be absorbed into the mainstream. The intimation is that they should be absorbed to the point of losing all identity.

As a *poshrat* myself (a half-blood Romany), and a lover of all that makes the Gypsy life so different from others, I would like to help the pendulum swing back a little, returning to some of the romance of the Gypsies. By this, I do not attempt to deny the reality of today's Gypsy situation (not, necessarily, the "Gypsy Problem"), but merely choose to focus on the more positive aspects in an attempt to maintain a balance.

Whatever the state of Gypsy life today, in the past theirs has been a colorful lifestyle: living in brightly painted *vardos* and *benders*, cooking over campfires, moving about the countryside while scraping together an existence and living by their wits. In my lifetime, growing up in England since the mid-1930s, I witnessed the gradual disappearance of the travelers in that country. Today, nearing the end of the twentieth century, there is only one English Rom family, to my knowledge, that still lives entirely by "the old ways." There are others who still travel the roads, yes, but they have adopted modern conveniences (including portable television sets). Most of these families have abandoned the old horse-drawn wagons for sleek, shiny motorhomes.

As an ethnic people, the Gypsies are disappearing. Shortly after World War II, authorities in Britain forced the travelers to place their children in schools, and to keep them in any one for at least one year. This immediately precludes traveling the roads throughout the year in their time-honored tradition, so Gypsies are being forced to take up permanent residence somewhere. If they do attempt to travel, they are oppressed by harassment from petty local officials enforcing laws, and by laws seemingly designed to single out the travelers. Racial discrimination is prevalent. As Pierre Derlon says (*Secrets of the Gypsies*, New York: Ballantine, 1977), "Bureaucracy, the police state, national fanaticism, and a narrow shopkeeping mentality are getting the better of the last of the 'free men.' There was a time when the only things that mattered to the gypsy were his own integrity, his tribe, the few square feet of earth on which he slept, and the roof of starlit sky which covered him. He had a harsh awakening." Harsh indeed!

My intention in this book is to recapture some of the past before it is lost and gone forever. If I seem to romanticize, it is done intentionally, that this aspect should not be lost. The Gypsies were—and some few still are—a colorful people, individuals, with their own pride and dignity. It would be a shame if they were absorbed to the point of extinction.

A Gypsy family in camp.

1

PROCESSION:
Exodus and Spread

That the Gypsy people originated in northern India is now firmly established. What is not established, and may never be, is what prompted the mass exodus from that area and the exact date that it started. Elwood Trigg (*Gypsy Demons and Divinities*. Seacaucus, NJ: Citadel, 1973) says:

> It is sufficient to make the hypothesis that a thousand years after the appearance of the Aryan peoples in northern India, the area was continually invaded by successive armies of first the Greeks, then the Persians, Scythians and Kushites. In the later era, both the Huns and Mohameddans also invaded the area. It would seem that the incessant military and political turmoil which these successive invasions caused to northwestern India succeeded in dislodging certain tribes of people which have come to be known as gypsies. It is possible that these people, forced to become sedentary by their conquerers, moved west in hope of retaining their nomadic way of life.

Whatever the reason, at some time in the middle of the ninth or tenth century large groups of people departed their homeland and moved westward. They passed through Pakistan, Afghanistan, and Persia, eventually reaching the Caspian Sea, north of the Persian Gulf. There they split into at least two distinct groups, one going northward through Turkey and, by way of Byzantium, into Bulgaria; the other, smaller band, going southward, sweeping down through Jordan into Egypt.

By 1348 the nomads were in Serbia, with others heading north through Walachia and into Moldavia. By the turn of that century they were to be found as widely spread as in Peloponnesus and Corfu in the south; Bosnia, Transylvania, Hungary, Bohemia; and, in the early 1400s, into Central Europe: Rome, Barcelona, Orleans, Hildesheim, and Paris. The group from the south traveled through Egypt, across the north of Africa and, crossing the Straits of Gibraltar, advanced through Spain to reach Granada. In 1417 there were travelers in Germany and by 1430 they had reached England and Wales.

From their swarthy skin and colorful dress, some observers decided that these mysterious people must be descendants of the ancient Egyptians! The idea caught on; they began to be referred to as "the Egyptians," later shortened to "the 'Gyptians" and then to "the 'Gypsies." (They also became known, at different times and in different places, as Bohemians, Tartars, Moors, and even Saracens. In fact they were a mixture of the various northern Indian tribes: Jats, Nats, Dards, Sindis, and Doms.)The earliest record of the Romany— from *Rom,* meaning a male Gypsy—in the north of Great Britain is found in an account ledger of the Lord High Treasurer of Scotland, recording a payment of £7 "to the Egyptian's (by) the King's command..." dated April 22, 1505. Soon account ledgers throughout the United Kingdom began showing payments made to "Gypcy" entertainers and to the "Egypcions."

The sudden appearance of these thousands of nomads across Europe caused some consternation. Just who were they? Where had they come from? The Gypsies themselves played up the idea of their having come from "Little Egypt," as they called it. It didn't take long for them to produce documents proclaiming that they traveled under the patronage of the Pope, the Emperor of Germany, and various other rulers and influential people. They claimed, among other things, that they had been given permission to wander and beg alms. Since this was a time when the Church had elevated charity into a virtue, the Rom were able to live very well!

One common story was that the Gypsies were living out a seven-year penance imposed on them because of their paganism. They would settle into an area and happily live off their neighbors' charity. But then, when several times the seven years had passed and they were still there, the local populace began to smell a rat.

The nomads scraped out a living as singers and dancers, gradually capitalizing on their looks and their mysterious air by practicing palm-reading and other forms of divination. The public was intrigued, and soon the occult arts became a major Romany practice. They also had some skill in animal handling and in metalcraft. Indeed, the Byzantine Gypsies enjoyed a metallurgical monopoly for a while.

Having outlived their welcome in many areas, however, they became regarded, by the authorities at least, as undesirables. Jean-Paul Clébert (in *The Gypsies*, London: Penguin Books, 1967) quotes the "General Inventory of the History of Thieves" that said:

> ...to be considered as an outstanding robber, it was necessary to...know all the tricks and wiles and activities of the Gypsies....

The Gypsies had earned a reputation as thieves, a reputation that still taints them today. Yet the reputation was somewhat undeserved, at least in the beginning. It came about from the Gypsy philosophy that everything that exists does so for the pleasure and delight of human kind. They believe the trees and flowers, the birds and beasts are all here for our enjoyment. Consequently, when a Gypsy passed along a road and saw an apple tree bearing fruit, he would think nothing of stopping and helping himself to this bounty. Similarly, to trap a rabbit or a pheasant for food was to enjoy that which the gods provided. How, the Gypsy reasoned, could a man or farmer or landowner object to this, for surely no man can own that which is given freely by the gods? So the travelers helped themselves to what others saw as their property. It was no wonder that, in their innocence, the Gypsies earned a reputation as thieves.

That innocence did not last long. Later, and in the present day, thievery is a result of fighting to exist, rather than being due to any earlier philosophies.

So began the persecutions from which the Gypsy people have still not freed themselves. Throughout Europe they had become a major social problem, especially since it was virtually impossible to force them into a sedentary (as opposed to migratory) way of life. King Ferdinand of Spain, in 1492, banished them from his country. Any who would not leave, he said, should be exterminated! To again quote Clébert:

> People of fixed residence...regarded all those of itinerant occupations who had no settled abode

and came from distant countries as possessed of
the evil eye...all the more if he had a swarthy face,
wore rings in his ears, lived in "wheeled houses,"
and spoke a language which was obviously not a
Christian one.

The Gypsies were equated with Witches and sorcerers; they were
accused of engaging in black magic and dealing with the Devil. In
1539 the French Parliament, joined in 1560 by the States General of
Orléans, called on "all those imposters known by the name of
Bohemians or Egyptians to leave the kingdom under penalty of the
galleys." In Britain, Henry VIII had issued a similar edict in 1531. By
1572 they had been forced out of Venice and Milan. Sweden ejected
them in 1662.

Happily for the Gypsies, effective enforcement of these various
edicts was lax. In addition, the "mysterious Egyptians" had gained
many supporters among the local population. The Rom frequently
managed to sink unobtrusively into the background, for a while at
least. By the late eighteenth century the Gypsies were still in place
over most of western Europe—in place and growing. Purposeless
brutality toward them was finally seen as a waste of energy. Gradually new suggestions were heard on how to accept this colorful people.
For a time, Britain, France and Spain attacked the problem by
deporting the Gypsies, thus actually helping them in their spread
around the world. Britain sent them to Australia and to the New
World, France sent them to Louisiana, and Spain sent them to Brazil.

As recently as the mid-twentieth century the Gypsies were still
being savagely persecuted. In World War II the Nazis set up in
France, alone, eleven concentration camps just for Gypsies. At least a
quarter of a million Gypsies died in the death camps. Some say the
total number of Gypsies that died, from all countries under German
control, could be as high as 600,000.

In Germany, in the mid-eighteenth century, reform was seen as
the answer to the "Gypsy problem." Forced reform, that was, and religion was seen as the most effective tool of that reform. Missionaries
were sent out to mingle with the Gypsies and especially to work on
their children. Continuous forced religious conversion was to have a

final effect. A parallel might well be seen with the conversion to Christianity forced on many Native American tribes. Ed McGaa, Eagle Man, in *Mother Earth Spirituality* (San Francisco: Harper-Row, 1990), says:

> The Bureau of Indian Affairs, a federal agency, worked hand in hand with the (Christian) missionaries to subvert and destroy native ways... the great majority of Indian youth were educated in boarding schools, separated from their parents for most of their developmental years, in the names of education, assimilation, and proselytizing salvation....Indian religion...was regarded as heathen and pagan, with no value relative to one's spiritual growth. Indian youth, used to being very close to not only their parents, but also their grandmothers and grandfathers, aunts and uncles, their *tiyospaye*, were abruptly separated at the age of six from this close relationship and cast into an alien, cold, unnatural institution, devoid of the natural warmth and closeness that the *tiyospaye* provided so well.

Many Native American tribes were forbidden to speak their own language, to engage in their ethnic dances or any form of religious worship. The Bureau of Indian Affairs could well have taken a page from Gypsy history, for that is exactly what was done to the travelers in many countries of the world in the eighteenth, nineteenth, and even the twentieth centuries. Trigg states:

> This close association between legal oppression and forced religious conversion was to have a profound impact upon the gypsy mind regarding the attitudes toward non-gypsy religious convictions. In some cases it would mean that gypsies would hold ever more closely to their own magico-religious concepts while often adopting only superficially those convictions of the surrounding society which they considered necessary for survival.

That the Gypsies did "hold...to their own magico-religious con-
cepts" is set forth in this book. In recent years I have gathered
together information on the beliefs and practices of many of the
Rom, mainly from England but from other countries as well. There
are certain things which I am not allowed to say, but much is here
presented in *Gypsy Witchcraft & Magic*.

2

PATHS TO DEITY:
Religious Beliefs and Practices

The Gypsies' original religious beliefs were pagan but over their many centuries of wanderings, they have assimilated a blend of pagan and non-pagan (Jewish and Christian) teachings and beliefs. Wherever the Gypsies rested in their travels, they would adopt—at least outwardly—the religious beliefs of their immediate neighbors, so that there would be no conflict. Sir Edward Evans-Pritchard once said (in his preface to Trigg's *Gypsy Demons*): "Gypsies have had to assume for protection the guise of Hindus, Moslems and Christians, a cloak not uncommon among minorities. But a cloak for protection does not mean total pretense." However strong these outward expressions of religion seemed to outsiders, certain beliefs remained strong within the Gypsies, and certain rites and ceremonies have passed on down to the present day. Elwood Trigg suggests that Christianity has, in fact, "unwittingly provided a means by which gypsy magical practices and beliefs have managed to survive under the guise and respectability of the Church." He goes on to say: "Essentially they are a free-spirited people in more ways than one. Normally nomadic in lifestyle, they have reserved the right to be able to pick and choose what they feel is best and most beneficial for themselves whether the choice is between places in which to live or faiths in which to believe."

There are hints—in the mythology of the Gypsies of Central Asia, for example—that there was once veneration of the sun, in the person of the sun god Obertsshi. The moon was also regarded as a god in some areas, and as Alako by the Scandinavian Gypsies. At the full moon whole tribes of Gypsies would gather together to celebrate. Weddings were held at this time, as were baptisms. The full moon was, and in many areas still is, a time for celebration and—as we will see later in this book—a time for the working of magic.

Chanti, the Festival of Ganesha, the Indian elephant-headed deity, is a sun celebration. Western Gypsies celebrate it around the time of Lughnasadh, the Wiccan August Eve Sabbat (some celebrate it as *Shanti*, at the summer solstice). It is considered extremely unlucky to look directly at the moon during this celebration.

Phallus worship has been attributed to the Gypsies. It is, of course, a common form of worship throughout much of India, the original homeland of the Gypsies, with the cult of Shiva and veneration of both the lingam (male organ) and yoni (female organ). Phallicism exists in many primitive religions and has done so throughout history—the phallus being regarded as a symbol of fertility. Yugoslavian Gypsies term the male sexual organ the *kar*. Trigg says, "So sacred is the kar...that it is incorporated into (the Gypsies') prayers" (*Gypsy Demons,* 1973).

Charles Godfrey Leland (1824–1903), the first president of the Gypsy Lore Society, in his book *Gypsy Sorcery and Fortune Telling* (London: Fisher-Unwin, 1891), mentions a goddess of the Gypsies named Gana, whom he associates with Diana. I have found mention of Gana with Rom in two areas of England. Also similar to Diana, in name at least, is Dina of the Wallachina Gypsies.

A Romany child, they believe, is born into a world of powerful forces, both positive and negative, good and evil. As soon as possible after birth the child must be "baptised"; that is, it must be ceremonially sprinkled with salt water and named. (Many also fumigate the child with incense, as do today's Wiccans and others.) In Scandinavia, a large fire is built at the mouth of the birthing tent. Its purpose is to hold at bay any evil entities until such time as the child has been consecrated. Throughout his or her life, the Gypsy child will be constantly aware of the struggle between good and evil that exists on earth.

Christian baptism would sometimes be accepted, but for reasons the Church would hardly smile upon. In *Gypsies: Wanderers of the World* (Bart McDowell, Washington, D.C.: National Geographic Society, 1970), Gypsy Cliff Lee is reported as saying: "I went to church often, but only to baptisms. The priests used to give a baptized child a bit of money. I recall once when I was a boy we went to eight churches one Sunday and got the same infant baptized each time. Different names in every church. A borrowed baby." So even the newly born can generate an income!

The Romany, despite being incredibly chauvanistic, religiously seem to prefer to worship the female rather than the male. Their "Saint" is known as "Black Sara," or "Sara *la Káli*," but differs in many respects from the Saint Sara of the Catholic Church. There are actually two legends. In one legend, Sara, an Egyptian, was the maidservant of Mary Salome and Mary Jacobe (mothers of Saints James and John, and relatives of Mary Magdalene), traveling with them. After a bad storm, Sara guides them, by the stars, to the far distant shore.

In the other, more interesting, legend, Sara was a Gypsy camped at the shore when the saints' boat approached. The telling, according to Franz de Ville (*Tziganes,* Brussels 1956), is as follows:

> One of our people who received the first Revelation was Sara the Kali. She was of noble birth and was chief of her tribe on the banks of the Rhone. She knew the secrets that had been transmitted to her....The Rom at that period practiced a polytheistic religion, and once a year they took out on their shoulders the statue of Ishtari (Astarte) and went into the sea to receive benediction there. One day Sara had visions which informed her that the Saints who had been present at the death of Jesus would come, and that she must help them. Sara saw them arrive in a boat. The sea was rough, and the boat threatened to founder. Sara threw her dress on the waves, and, using it as a raft, she floated towards the Saints and helped them reach land.

The Gypsies call her Sara "*la Kâli,*" which means both "the black woman" and "the Gypsy woman," in Romanes (the Gypsy language). A statue of Sara is kept where the two Marys were supposed to have landed, in the crypt of the church at Saintes Maries de la Mer, on the Ile de la Camargue, at the mouth of the Rhone River. Every year thousands of Gypsies make a pilgrimage to the church. Only the Rom had the right to enter the crypt, until 1912, but now anyone and everyone squeezes in there. Clébert describes the crypt: "...on the left, as one enters, there is an old altar, the pagan altar (some say that it was for bull-sacrifice in the worship of Mithra, but of this there is no proof); in the center there is the Christian third-century altar; and, to the right, there is the statue of Sara" (*The Gypsies,* 1967). Part of the pilgrimage takes place on the morning of May 25. A great procession winds its way to the sea, where the statue is symbolically submerged, as Clébert says, "in the manner of all cults of the great goddesses of fecundity."

The Romany word for God is *Duvvel* (*Devel* or *Del*, among some groups) and the Devil is *Ben* (or *Bengh*). God is thought of in terms of being the sun, moon, sky, clouds, and stars, rather than anthropomorphically. In the same way, the Devil is more of a negative force than an actual all-evil deity.

The *Kalderash* Gypsies say that God is not creator of the world. They say that the world has always existed, as the mother of us all. They refer to the earth as *De Develeski*—the Divine Mother.

The *Nagas* are the Asian equivalent of mer-folk (originally meaning "sea people"). In ancient times, people believed that the mer-folk had bodies that were either half-human and half-fish or, sometimes, half-snake. They are semi-divine beings who control the weather and, hence, can bring rain. They typically live in great palaces in the ocean, or at the bottom of rivers, lakes and ponds, where they guard great treasures. If crossed or insulted they can be vengeful, but when befriended can confer great blessings. They like offerings of milk, coins, and food, which Gypsies leave at the base of a tree, near water, or by a sacred well.

There are certain ethnic groups within the Gypsies. The Kalderash is one such group. Other main groups are the *Gitanos* and the *Manush*. The Kalderash are metalworkers—tinsmiths, coppersmiths, etc. The Gitanos are found mainly in the South of France, Spain, Portugal, and North Africa. The Manush, or *Manouches*, specialize in animal training and are often traveling showmen and circus people. Angus Fraser (*The Gypsies*, Blackwell, 1992) examines the various Gypsy groupings at some length. Jean-Paul Clébert says that most divisions are arbitrary, with each group claiming to be the only true Gypsies and despising the others! Clébert says that mixed marriages, between the groups, are rare.

There are many sub-divisions of Gypsies: the *Blidari, Rudari*, and *Lingurari* who make all types of wooden articles (the Blidari specializing in objects for the home); *Ciobatori*, who are cobblers, making footwear; *Costorari*, the tinsmiths; *Ghilabari*, the musicians; *Lautari*, makers of musical instruments; *Meshteri Lacatuschi*, locksmiths; *Salahori*, masons and bricklayers; *Vatraschi*, gardeners; and *Zlatari*, goldsmiths. Spellings may vary in different areas, but these names are generally recognized.

The vardo is the Gypsy family's home-on-wheels. It is a wagon that, in Britain and many other parts of the world, is brilliantly carved and decorated. Horse-drawn, it contains all the family's possessions (see Chapter 3). The whole family sleeps in the vardo, although in good weather it is not uncommon for them to construct a bender for the children to sleep in.

Neither birth nor death should pollute the home, according to the Gypsies. Births take place in a bender, the Gypsy homemade tent, set up away from the vardo. Women move into a bender for births and the sick and elderly move into one for death. No self-respecting Gypsy would be caught dying in a bed in the vardo.

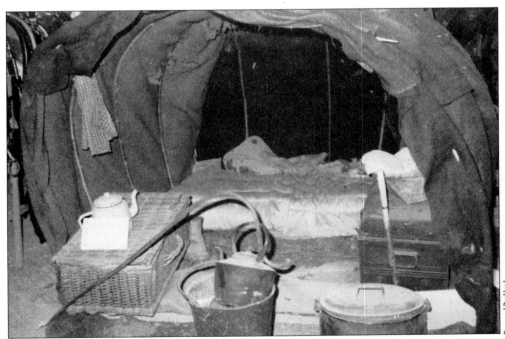

A bender tent provides shelter for the Gypsy family. Births and deaths take place in the bender so these life events will not pollute the vardo.

Preparation for death can take place with the cooperation of the dying. While still hanging on to life, they are washed with salt water and dressed in new clothes. The women are usually dressed in a large number of skirts (five seems to be a special number). In this way the dying are reassured that they are properly prepared for their final journey. Their family will gather about the dying person and eat, drink, and talk quite normally. But when death is announced there is great crying and even screaming, with a tremendous display of genuine sorrow. This may go on well into the night, but eventually it gives way to chanting and singing.

After death the body is placed in a coffin and the deceased's jewelry and some gold coins are placed in the coffin with the body. Many times ordinary items such as a knife and fork, or the deceased's favorite pipe and/or violin, may also be put in the coffin. At the burial, beer, wine, or rum is spilled on the coffin and, later, on the grave, as a libation. The salutation *"Tutti sutti mishto"* ("May you sleep well") is given, then Gypsy musicians play as the coffin is lowered into the ground. Burial frequently takes place in some secret place, known only to close family members. It may be in a favorite section of woods, or in the corner of some field or wild place. There is no apparent grave marker, although a bramble bush may be encouraged to grow over it, to keep animals from desecrating the grave.

Years ago, in many parts of England, when the head of a family died, the body would be placed in his or her vardo, along with all their possessions, and the whole thing set on fire. The rest of the family would then be taken in to live with relatives. There seems to be a parallel with the Egyptian and other cultures' practice of burying the dead with all that might be needed in the afterlife. In 1950 I remember watching a BBC television report of such a Gypsy burning. I was surprised to hear that it was a Buckland Gypsy who was being cremated in their vardo. At that time it was announced that this was probably the last time such a burning would take place. Today, with vardos being sold to collectors for eighty to a hundred thousand dollars or more, it would certainly be unusual to burn one.

Attitudes vary, but in general there is a fear of the dead. Gypsies are great believers in ghosts and want to run no risk of a departed spirit attaching itself, in some way, to the living! This may be part of the reason for burning a vardo—with their home and possessions gone there is nothing to draw back the dead person. In fact, the name of the deceased is no longer spoken, for fear of drawing back him or her.

Some Gypsies do not believe in an afterlife while others—German Gypsies, for example—believe in reincarnation. In this latter belief, the spirit will return to earth three times, in different bodies, with 500 earthly years passing between each appearance. Serbian Gypsies believe in an afterlife much like this earthly life, but with no "death" at the end of it.

There is an old saying that if you ask ten different Gypsies the same question you will get ten different answers. And, if you ask just one Gypsy the same question ten times, you will still get ten different answers! So it seems to be with many Romany beliefs, such as in life after death. Gypsies in different areas, and even in different families/tribes, hold different beliefs.

The Romany word for ghost, or spirit, is *mullo*. This word can also refer to the "living dead"—to vampires. There is a strong possibility that someone (Gypsy) who has died has done so as the result of evil influence. After becoming a mullo the deceased person will attempt to track down the person who caused his or her death. Despite beliefs such as this, Gypsies will not hesitate to sleep in a cemetery, if necessary. This is because they believe that only the Gypsy dead become vampires. *Gaujos* (or *gorgios*), or non-Gypsies, do not, so there is nothing to fear from their ghosts. Trigg speaks of the mullo's insatiable need for sexual intercourse, to the extent that his widow is often driven to a state of exhaustion (*Gypsy Demons and Divinities*. Seacaucus, NJ: Citadel, 1973). He says:

> In some instances, vampires have been known to return in order to have sexual intercourse with the woman they were never allowed to marry in life. In some cases, the vampire may ask this woman to return with him to his grave-world for

the remainder of eternity. In some instances, too, a vampire, whether married or not, may return in order to have sex with any woman he may choose. Indeed, in some instances young women are believed to have had long romances with men whom they later came to discover were vampires. Some gypsies claim that such vampire lovers are visible only to those with whom they are having sex.

In Slavic countries there is a Gypsy belief in werewolves. Some people think that anyone who has led an especially evil life will become a werewolf, while others think that werewolves are the result of a victim having the blood sucked from him, or her, by evildoers. Such a victim will gradually lose the power of speech and, during nighttime hours, will be transformed into a wolf to go and serve the evildoer.

As mentioned earlier, from the fifteenth century at least, Gypsies have been identified with witches and sorcerers. The Rom had, more or less of necessity in order to earn a living, fostered the belief that they possessed certain arcane knowledge and were adepts in the occult arts. This was to backfire on them in many areas where they were subsequently believed to be trafficking with the devil. For example, when Gypsies worked with trained animals, it seemed obvious to onlookers that the dog walking on its hind feet (for example) was nothing more than an imp of the devil in the Gypsy's care!

Clébert makes a very good point when he suggests that Gypsies were frequently confused with witches through the then-popular conception of witches' sabbats. It was common knowledge that such sabbats were held in the woods or at a crossroads. Occasionally villagers, traveling late at night, might stumble upon a group of Gypsies in a clearing in the woods, or camped at the crossroads, who were playing their music and eating and drinking after a day of traveling the highways. To the villager, hurrying along in fear of witches, these were witches' sabbats he was seeing! Clébert elaborates on the Gypsy dancing and music, saying that it approximates that of witches'. He quotes De Lancre's *Tableau de l'Inconstance des Mauvais Anges* (1613): "...violins, trumpets and tambourines which produced great

Jallin' a Drom (Traveling the Road).

harmony; and at the said gatherings there is extreme pleasure and rejoicing..." and commenting, "It is hard to blame me for wishing to compare them with the classic dances of the *Gitanes* (Spanish Gypsies) which still seem to strangers to be the most exact representation of sensual pleasure" (*The Gypsies,* 1967).

Whether or not any Gypsies shared Wiccan beliefs, we do not know. There is no doubt that there was much similarity between the two groups. Witches had a vast knowledge of herbs, for example. Gypsies had a similar knowledge. Their nomadic lifestyle brought them into close proximity with all the herbs and wildflowers of the back roads and lanes. They developed herbal remedies to doctor their own people, then dispensed them as magical elixirs to needy villagers. They had a closeness with nature that the witches also possessed, and may even have worshipped the same deities under different names.

On the steps of her *vardo* home, this Gypsy girl worked on a wooden flower stand to sell to the *gaujos*. (Photographed in the Boswell Camp at Lock's Bottom, Orpington, Kent, England, in October 1912.)

A gathering of Gypsies at the *atchin' tan*, or campsite. This is a group of Galician Gypsies, known for their metalwork, especially working with copper. (Photographed at The Kursaal, Southend-on-sea, Essex, England, in June 1914.)

Smiths and Careys making pegs (clothes pins) and drying grass. These families traveled in the bow-topped *waggon* shown here (upper left) and would set up a bender tent (far right of photo) for extra space. (Scott Macfie Albums, Lock's Bottom, Orpington, Kent, England.)

Sharpening knives and scissors was a good way to make a living. Here Charley (Moti) Lovell makes ready with his sharpening outfit. Behind him is a small *bender* tent, used for additional living quarters in the Gypsy camp. (Photographed near Llangefni, Gwynd, Wales, in 1914.)

The burning of Helen Shevlin's *vardo* at her death in 1933. All of her belongings would have been placed inside to be consumed, thus ending her total existence. Her name would no longer be mentioned by her family and friends.

Brough Hill Fair in Yorkshire, Westmorland (Cumbria), England, in 1913. This is one of the regular gathering points for travelers. The neighboring Appleby Horse Fair is the oldest, largest, and best known of such gatherings. Gypsies from all over Great Britain travel to these and similar sites.

This beautiful Ledge-style *vardo* was the home of George, Berti, Rodi (née Wainwright), and Jim Heron. It is lavishly decorated with carvings. (Photographed in the Cumbria vicinity of England in 1911.)

Construction of a *bender* tent (see Chapter 15). The temporary shelter is constructed from hazelnut branches. Behind the *bender* is a bow top *vardo* in which the Gypsy family traveled. (Photographed near Carnarvon, Gwynd, Wales, in 1914.)

A Gypsy mother washing clothes in front of *bender* tents.

Orni and Levi Carey and their son Harry making *kipsies* (baskets) and beehives to sell. (Photographed near Sevenoaks, Kent, England.)

Gypsy *raklies* (young women). They help the older women with the chores, and with looking after the *chavvies* (children). (Photographed at Birkenhead in 1911.)

Burning of an old Gypsy's living *waggon* after his funeral. This is no longer a practice, with *vardos* selling to collectors for up to $100,000.

Two older Coppersmith women photographed at Wandsworth in August 1911. Many Gypsy women smoke cigars and/or pipes. The matriarch of the tribe is known as the *puri dai*.

The strong arm of the law? British "Bobbies" lead away a Gypsy woman and her child as they attempt to clear a Gypsy encampment. This was part of the ongoing harassment of the travelers, still going on today.

The interior of Gildroy Gray's bow-topped *vardo*, photographed in the vicinity of The Red Well, near Carnforth, Lancashire, England, in 1916.

Matthew Wood, with his knife-sharpening barrow, photographed near Bala, Merionethshire, in 1914.

3

THE GYPSY MYSTERIES:

Growth of a Reputation

The Gypsies were, and largely still are, nomads. They were constantly on the move. Even when establishing themselves in Europe, they would stay in one area for only a certain time before moving on to another area.

The English Gypsies of the last and present century would travel for most of the year, but camp in one locality throughout the whole of the winter. Often, in the winter, several different branches of a family or tribe would come together after being separated the rest of the year. There they would catch up on family news and gossip. With the coming of spring they would all take to the roads again, going their different ways. Certain sites were popular with particular Gypsy families where, perhaps, a good relationship had been established with the land owner and where they knew they were welcome each year. Sometimes the resting place was determined by the time of year. For example, in early June the Horse Fair is held at Appleby-in-Westmorland, Cumbria (the big sale day is usually the second Wednesday of the month), so any Gypsy family interested in horse trading (and that seems to cover most of them!) will make sure that their travels bring them to Appleby at that time of the year. This is the largest of such fairs. There are other smaller horse fairs around the country—Barnaby Fair, Brigg Fair, Lee Gap Fair, for example—that also attract the horse-traders. Those who earn money with sideshows, or who work carnivals, will head for the sites of major fun fairs such as the Nottingham Goose Fair in October. Many will go to Kent for the hop harvest, and so on. The usual mode of travel was the horse-drawn wagon, although today the motor home has taken over almost completely.

The Gypsy wagon—their home on wheels—was an elaborately decorated affair. Variations are found throughout Europe and even in America, but it is the English wagon, or vardo, which is best known. The vardos reached their prime in the late nineteenth century and early part of the twentieth century. Up until World War II it was common to see lines of vardos moving slowly along the country lanes and even on the major roads of England, Wales, and Scotland.

The vardo is a one-room house. It has a stove for cooking and warmth, a bed, and closets. It has a door (except in the case of the "Open Lot" shown below) and windows. The door is at the front (with one exception) and there is a tailgate, or cratch, at the back. Under this rack is an enclosed box, known as the pan-box, for holding cooking pots and pans that might be soot-covered. Other boxes, chicken coops, and other paraphernalia may also be hung from hooks under the chassis. The whole wagon is light enough that it can be pulled by one horse.

There are different types of vardos. The most basic is the OPEN LOT, a flat wagon with hoops that hold up a curved, tent-like, canvas top (see photo on page 25). The rear is a fixed wooden wall with a small window in it. The front is an open frame, hence its name, with a curtain across. The bow roof extends slightly in front and rear to form slight porches. As in all vardos, the stove is at the front, on the left as you enter, its chimney sticking up through the roof. The bed is built across the rear wall.

An Open Lot Vardo.

The BOW TOP looks similar to the Open Lot, but it has an enclosed front, with a split door and window(s). A SQUARE BOW has a canvas top also, but instead of being drawn over bent hoops the canvas goes straight up the sides, then straight across the top. This vardo has a door at the front.

More solid looking, perhaps, are the READING, LEDGE, BURTON, and other similar vardos. They are built with wooden, windowed walls, and are enclosed front and rear. Frequently they have Mollicroft skylights in their slightly bowed roofs and one or two windows on each side. Removable steps that clip onto the front footboard are stowed under the cratch for traveling. The sides are built of "penny boarding" (boards the width of the old English penny) over a basic frame. The wheels are large; sometimes the front ones are smaller in diameter than the rear. The average vardo is about ten feet in length and weighs about 3,000 pounds.

The most striking thing (to the gaujo) about a Romany vardo is its decoration. Vardos are elaborately carved and then intricately painted in bright colors, highlighted with gold leaf. Reds, greens, and yellows are used, but never black. One of the few craftsmen left who can do this work is Peter Ingram, himself a Romany, who lives and works in Hampshire, England. (C. H. Ward-Jackson and Denis E. Harvey have written what is probably the definitive book on the vardo, *The English Gypsy Caravan—Its Origins, Builders, Technology and Conservation* [Devon, Newton Abbot: David & Charles, 1972].)

On the roads today you may see a large motor home with a small car being towed behind it. Obviously this second vehicle is for running around in, after the motor home has been set up on its campsite. The Gypsies have a similar idea. Their "runabout" is a light, two-wheeled cart, called a FLAT CART or Trap. It is frequently decorated as splendidly as a vardo. In a pinch, small hoops can be stuck in the sides of the Flat Cart and a canvas thrown over them to make an "accommodation top" for overnight sleeping (see illustration on page 157).

An Open Lot Vardo has an open front end. It will usually have curtains that can be drawn to keep out wind and rain.

Raymond Buckland

Raymond Buckland

Author Raymond Buckland (left) and friend Peter Ingram stand beside an Open Lot Vardo.

A Bow Top Vardo is enclosed at the front end, with double doors and windows to protect occupants from the weather.

A Bradford Flat Cart, owned by coach painter Peter Ingram. Several generations of the Ingram family were builders and painters of Vardos and coaches.

This lavishly decorated wagon is a Ledge Vardo.

Interior detail of a Ledge Vardo (below). Note the intricate carvings and the angel lamp.

The author looks out from the open upper doors of a Bow Top Vardo.

A modern Showman's Wagon.

Another contemporary adjunct to the motor home is the tent. Again the Gypsies were way ahead of modern-day campers. To supplement their living quarters, they would build a "bender" tent. They cut long, flexible, branches, stuck one end into the ground, in two long lines, and threaded the other end through holes in a central wooden, ridge pole. Hazelnut branches were preferred, since they bend easily. The whole thing was covered with tarps or blankets (see Chapter 15), making a very serviceable shelter. A fire could be built inside for warmth if an opening was made for the smoke to escape.

The Gypsy lifestyle was decidedly romantic to other eyes. Those eyes did not necessarily see the dust and dirt from traveling the roads and from lack of water, or the squalor frequently forced on the Rom by exclusion from all but the meanest of camping sites. Their romantic image was enhanced by the colorful wagons, the equally colorful dress: bright skirts, blouses, and headscarves for the women, and almost equally bright shirts and scarves for the men.

A Bradford Flat Cart, on the track at the Appleby Horse Fair.

The travelers were happy to encourage the awe they frequently found directed at them. They lived close to nature—as close as it was possible to get—and by virtue of that, they never lost the psychic connection that we all once enjoyed. Civilization and sophistication, despite their many benefits, have parted us from our natural attunement with metaphysical matters, but the Gypsies keep that connection and frequently use it, out of necessity, to earn a living.

It has been said that the Gypsy does not use his or her occult knowledge to help another Gypsy. This is true. Why? Not because of any fraudulence; not because the Gypsies don't believe in what others think they possess. It is simply because *all* Gypsies have the capability, so it is not necessary to use it for others in the same way that they would use it for a gaujo. Instead, the Rom use it for those non-Gypsies who have lost the gift. The practice of the occult arts by the Gypsies has provided them with a more or less endless source of revenue, while at the same time nurturing the gaujos' awe, a combination of respect and fear for these unique people.

The linking, in the Middle Ages, of Gypsies with witches and sorcerers was not entirely incorrect. Gypsies have a knowledge that, discounting their Romany background, would be classed as "Hedge Witchcraft," that is, the witchcraft of the old pagan people. It differs from that of today's Wicca in that there is no emphasis on the religious side. The emphasis—or lack thereof—is on using herbal lore, basic magic, and divination as part of everyday life. None of it is regarded as special; simply as a part and parcel of living. Knowledge of herbs for cooking, for healing, for thurification; divination and argury for help in decision-making; spells and charms to direct events—this is the makeup of the Gypsy mysteries.

4

BIRTH OF THE SHUVANI:
The Gypsy Witch

The Romany word for "witch" is *shuvihani* (masculine *shuvihano*), sometimes shortened to *shuvani* and in some areas *shuv'ni*. (It is also sometimes spelled *chuvihani*.) It means a witch in the old sense of "wise one"—one knowledgeable in all aspects of the occult. Trigg says that the shuvanis "serve the important function in gypsy society of being able to both bless and curse, heal and make sick...the chuvihani is one who is respected for both wisdom and knowledge of magical beliefs and practices." She it is who also carries all the knowledge of the social taboos, and of the magically based rites and rituals, such as for baptism and marriage. Nowhere is the witch considered evil or repugnant in any way by Gypsies. With the travelers, she is simply someone with special knowledge and/or power that is used for good or bad, according to his or her desires.

Eric Maple, in *The Dark World of Witches* (London: Robert Hale, 1972), says:

> Historians have observed that there was a sudden revival of witchcraft and sorcery in the fifteenth century, and among the causes of this was no doubt the arrival of the gipsies. Some time towards the close of the fourteenth century this nomadic people arrived in Europe, probably from Asia, bringing with them magical practices which, in England, had long been concealed beneath a veneer of Christianity.

What Maple claims for England probably holds true for much, if not most, of Europe. There is certainly a very real possibility that the Gypsies' arrival may have been the spark that ignited the revival of paganism and the practice of magic.

There is no question that the Gypsies did more than anyone to disseminate a belief in the occult among the multitudes.

Leland quotes an old Romany poem:

> *Ki shan I Romani,*
> *Adoi san' I chov'hani*

32

Where Gypsies go,
There the witches are, we know.

Charlatans they may have been, in many ways, but not entirely
devoid of certain magical powers. Fraud, deceit, and imposture alone
could not have been their only stock in trade for so many centuries.
"Where there's smoke there must be fire" goes the old adage, and it
must hold true here. They were Keepers of the Ancient Mysteries
and, for centuries now, have been the dispensers of that knowledge
around the world, to those who would hear.

Clébert claims that shuvanis are created by the union of a young
Romany female and a water or earth spirit. He says these spirits have
"carnal union" with future witches (*The Gypsies,* 1967). Although I
find few, if any, Gypsies today who believe that such a union takes
place, it is true that many shuvanis do go through something similar
to the Native American vision quest, bringing realization and previ-
ously unknown knowledge. However, the vast majority are apprenticed to an old shuvani, and learn their trade that way.

There are many superstitions in Gypsy lore. Omens, taboos,
prophecy—they are all part of everyday life for the nomads. At the
root of it is a belief in spirits—spirits of the earth, water, air, forest,
and field. Shuvanis can, and do, communicate with these spirits. Of
the three main types, air spirits are very independent and would as
soon harm humans as help them. They certainly seem to delight in
leading humans astray! The earth spirits, on the other hand, are frequently described as "noble." They are friendly and give good
counsel. Water spirits can be of either kind. They can have their
good moods and help humans, or be vindictive and, if not evil, at
least unkind.

I met with a shuvani just outside the little town of Betws-y-Coed,
in North Wales. Betws-y-Coed, incidentally, is one of the many places
in Gwynedd where the fairies, or *Tylwyth Teg*, are seen on a regular
basis, by people in all walks of life.

Bregus Wood, the shuvani I spent time with, was in her eighties
when I first met her in 1990. She told me that she had been taught
the arts by her mother, starting at the age of seven. For the first two
or three years she was just taught the names and uses of wild flowers

and herbs, and their medicinal qualities. Later she went on to make salves and potions, simples, poultices, and powders. It seems she was a natural healer for, by the time Bregus was thirteen, her healing powers had become legendary and Gypsies traveled from all over the country to see her. From there, she said, it was natural to go on to supplement this healing gift by the laying on of hands (see Chapter 6) and then by using charms and spells (Chapters 5, 9, and 12). Her mother died when Bregus was thirty and, although relatively young, she became the tribe's shuvani.

Leland says, "Women excel in the manifestation of certain qualities which are associated with mystery and suggestive of occult influences or power." Indeed, there are far more shuvanis than there are shuvanos, though the latter are not unknown and are respected just as much as their female counterparts. Leland also says, "The magic of the Gypsies is not all deceit, though they deceive with it. They put faith themselves in their incantations, and practise them on their own account. And they believe that there are women, and sometimes men, who possess supernatural power, partly inherited and partly acquired" (*Gypsy Sorcery*, 1891).

Sometimes a certain birthmark will indicate that a child will be one of the wise ones. Some view these birthmarks as a sort of "stigmata," attributing them to some traumatic event that happened to either the father or mother just prior to the child's birth. For example, if the father had been kicked by a horse and the child was subsequently born with a horseshoe-shaped birthmark, this would be taken as the sign of a potential shuvani. The child would be raised as such and apprenticed to a knowledgeable elder. The mother, also, would be treated with great respect; as one writer put it: "looked upon as a 'mother goddess,' venerated like statues of the Virgin Mother" (Derlon, 1977).

There is no single "initiation ceremony" to make a person a shuvani or shuvano. It is a gradual training, whether tutored or self-taught. Learning can last a lifetime. (That being the case, don't rush through this book! Take your time. Read it and study it. At the back I give a bibliography of books about Gypsies, for those who would like to learn more.)

In this book, *you* will be learning many of the secrets of the shuvanis. You have the advantage of not having to learn everything by heart. (Not immediately, anyway. I hope many of you will continue to use this knowledge until it does become second nature.) You can dip into the book here and there, using whatever you need when you need it. It is your reference book for Gypsy witchcraft and magic.

I will start, in the next chapter, with love magic, since that is one of the most popular—seemingly the most needed—of magics. From there we will look at health and healing, then on to money matters, luck, and protection. In Chapter 10 I'll talk about the many forms of divination used by the Rom, then examine such magical aids as talismans and amulets. Sex has always been an important part of Gypsy life, recognized for the powerful energy that it is. The Rom have not shrunk from using its power for magical purposes. We'll have a look

A Shuvani at work.

at that in Chapter 12, followed by animal magic and healing. I'll finish up with details on the construction of some of the magical tools
used by the travelers, showing you how to make them in the traditional Gypsy fashion. Before I get into specifics, however, I'd like to
talk for a moment about magic generally, and the working of it.

All magic done by the Gypsies involves the use of things that are
natural, or that are found in nature. Seldom, if ever, do the Rom find
it necessary to buy something that is manufactured (other than
something simple like a knife or similar tool). This is because the
Gypsies are used to making do with what they have and with what
they can easily obtain. Not only that, but they have found that natural objects have much purer vibrations than those that are manufactured—especially those manufactured from synthetic materials.

In some instances it is necessary to search the roads, woods,
and fields for a considerable time to find the item that is just right
for your spell. That searching is all part of the magical working, for
the anticipation, and the slight tension, of the search helps build
the power which will be charged into the object when it is found
and used.

Never rush magic. Most magic needs to be done at the right
time, whether by the hour of the day or night, or by the time of the
month, so plan ahead for it. Don't try to work magic on the spur of
the moment; it will seldom be successful. Magic—successful
magic—depends upon energy, the energy of the person doing the
magic. That energy (or "power," or whatever you want to call it) is
absorbed into the tools that are made and used, into the words that
are said, into the actions performed, and into the directing of the
final product.

Always try to do positive magic. By that I mean make sure that
whatever you are doing will not harm anyone in any way. More than
that, make sure that what you do will not interfere with anyone else's
free will. This is particularly important in working love magic. So
often I'm approached by someone who is madly in love with someone else but he or she does not love them. "How can I make
him/her love me?" I'm asked. The answer is not so much that you
can't make them love you, but that you *shouldn't*. Just ask yourself—

would you like to be made to love someone you wouldn't naturally care for? Of course you wouldn't! I have emphasized this in my other books and will continue to do so.

Unfortunately—perhaps because of the way they have been treated over the centuries—the Gypsies, like many other people, do not seem to consider the above. As I've mentioned, a shuvani can, and does, curse as well as cure. They often think nothing of bending someone to their will. Although I personally do not go along with that, some of the spells and magic I have included in this book do not altogether follow the harm-none principles. Yet they are the way the Gypsies work and, as such, I have included them for the sake of completeness and authenticity. So, whatever you do, examine the spell and what it promises as a result, and see if it is possible to do it—perhaps modifying it slightly—following positive principles. Most things *can* be done in a positive way, if you just give them a little thought.

In Wicca there is a belief that whatever you do comes back three-fold. Do good to someone and it will return with three times the energy. By the same token, do harm to someone and that, too, will return in magnified form. This belief is a corollary of the one Wiccan law: *An' it harm none, do what thou wilt.* This means, basically, that you can do anything you like so long as you don't harm anyone. I very much subscribe to these beliefs.

I have seen, many times, the "threefold return" have effect, both in the positive sense and in the negative. So I urge you, in working the magic of the Gypsies, to bear this in mind, and do nothing that will either harm another or even interfere with that person's free will. To use another age-old maxim: Do unto others as you would have others do unto you.

Your state of mind, when working magic, is important. You should be calm and collected, able to focus on what you will, and able to control your emotions. Emotions play an important part.

It is often necessary to get yourself extremely emotional about what you are trying to achieve, but not so emotional that you lose control, for you want to be able to direct the emotional energy that you generate.

Concentration is important. You should be able to concentrate on one thing, and one thing only, to the exclusion of all else. In our ordinary, everyday lives, we may sit at a desk and work on insurance papers, for example, or a grocery list, or a lesson plan, but our mind may also be "bouncing around," thinking of the party we'll be going to that evening, or the movie we saw the night before. To concentrate is to have one thought, and one thought only, in your mind. That is important in magic. It can take a lot of practice, so start practicing!

Along with concentration is visualization. How good are you at visualizing things? If you think—*really* think—of a rose, can you see every aspect of it? Can you turn it around, slowly, *in your mind* and see the difference in the petals; see the gradation of the color; see the details of the leaves and the thorns on the stem? Can you make your mind "zoom in" to the center of the bloom and see the minute drops of moisture on the petals? This is what I mean by concentration and visualization. Again, it is something that can be learned by practice.

Cleanliness is another little-thought-of aspect of working magic. Gypsies are frequently thought of, by gaujos, as being "dirty" people. There's good reason for this. They frequently *are* dirty, from the pure act of traveling dusty roads. Water is often scarce. When it is found, using it for drinking and cooking is far more important than using it for washing. So, yes, they often are dirty, but in the sense of unwashed, rather than in the sense of exuding foul, putrescent, impurities. Their preference is most certainly to be washed; when they do find water in abundance—at a river or stream—they welcome the chance to immerse themselves and get rid of the grime of travel. So, when working magic, think of yourself as a Gypsy camped beside a stream! Make sure that you are clean, physically as well as mentally. Make it a practice to take a bath before working magic.

To speak of breathing as being one of the requirements for working magic may seem redundant. Of course, I mean correct breathing. The Rom do not do morning exercises, filling their lungs and then totally exhausting them in the manner I, and others, have described in books on psychic development. They do not even think about how they are breathing, I'm sure. But they are aware of the fact that to do magic, it's necessary to be able to concentrate (as I've mentioned above), and that to concentrate it is advantageous to be breathing smoothly and calmly. If you are agitated or overexerted, your breathing is full and heavy. Unconsciously or consciously, your mind is drawn to the act of breathing, taking it away from other things, so calm your body and adopt a relaxed breathing style.

What about the place of work? Books on magic usually deal—often at great length—on the "temple" or "magic room" that will be used for working magic. Obviously the Gypsy is not a ceremonial magician. He or she has no extra room to spare. Like the Hedge Witch, the Gypsy does magic anywhere it can be done. It may be out in the woods, it may be in an open field, it may be in an old hut. Really, the place does not matter. Bregus Wood, the Welsh shuvani, would sometimes work in her old Bow Top vardo and sometimes beside the campfire outside it. Sometimes she would build a bender tent and do her magic in that, and sometimes she would go out and stand in the middle of a crossroads, where three country roads met. She told me that she has done what she termed her *"bok ta kushti bok booti"* (literally, her "bad and good luck work") everywhere, from sitting on a plow horse to lying underneath a vardo! As she said, "It's not where you do it, it's what you do!"

One of the attendant pleasures of magical ritual, for many people, is the "dressing up" in magical robes. Let's not dismiss this lightly. Ritual dress can be important and definitely has a place in magical preparation, even if that "ritual dress" is nothing more than a particular pair of jeans and a shirt worn for nothing else but that purpose. Just as it might behoove many would-be magicians to take a theatrical course in presentation (speech and gesture, stage presence, etc.), so it might also behoove them to study costume. Magically, choice of color is most important in attire, as is choice of material (silk, cotton, or linen, as opposed to nylon, rayon, or other synthetics). Clothing style—robes, tunic, shirt and pants or skirt, or nude—should be chosen to fit the type of magic to be performed.

I have seen an "ordinary" young man—one who would not normally draw a second glance—become a magnetic personality, simply by attiring himself in the robes of his magical order and assuming the demeanor of the practiced magician. To put on the dress of the magician is to put on the whole personality, to imbue oneself with the self-assuredness of the Mage. If this is so with most, if not all, magical practices, then it should be so with Gypsy magic also. Why not dress as a Gypsy? Many will jump at the opportunity or excuse, but in all seriousness, as outlined above, to dress the part is to live the part. There is probably no "typical" Gypsy dress; there is only the stereotypical dress.

Yet this is, in many places, remarkably accurate. The Rom seem to favor what they call "old fashioned" dress—the expression being a term of approval.

Women dress in long, voluminous skirts, full length or three-quarter length. These skirts are usually brightly colored, with multiple layers of petticoats underneath. In England, for many years, Scottish plaids were very much in favor. Tight bodices are common. Blouses—frequently low-cut—have full sleeves, puffed at the elbows and often trimmed with lace. Frequently an elaborately stitched and pleated apron (known as a *jodaka*), with a broad-fronted waistband, is worn. This is not a "kitchen" apron but is worn as a smart item of apparel (see Chapter 15). A silk scarf (*diklo*) may be worn over the hair, turban-style, or knotted under the chin, or it may be worn around the neck and fastened with a brooch. A shawl may be worn instead of, or in addition to, the diklo. Necklaces of amber and of jet are common, as is red coral. Shoes are often high-laced or buttoned boots with two-and-one-half-inch heels. Hair may be long and loose, or plaited and fastened with decorative clips. Gold jewelry is essential and much in evidence, rings being heavy. Silver is not worn much, except by the horses!

The men favor corduroy pants, usually of heavy wales, or heavy cloth, cut very high. They have a double-fronted fly with seven rows of stitching around the flap. They are cut close around the knees for ease in horseback riding. Coats are of heavy cloth, often dark green or brown, with a back belt and a yoke. The pockets are flapped, with four rows of stitching. There was always a deep "poacher's pocket" inside. The pants are fastened with horn buttons. Boots are sturdy, often riding boots. A broad-brimmed hat (*stardi*) is not uncommon. Shirts are frequently colored, though not as brightly as the women's. A large belt, the front looking like a girth strap, is worn in conjunction with suspenders. The Gypsy man, too, wears a diklo around his neck, usually of silk. Sometimes you'll see a Rom in a swallow-tail coat and wearing a vest. Again, solid gold jewelry is in evidence. Since Gypsies are forever on the move, banks are not of much use to them, so they carry their wealth with them, frequently in the form of jewelry.

A Gypsy man's vest, embellished with embroidery
and coins. Note the *diklo* worn at the throat.

From the point of view of magic working, you can use whatever you feel is "Gypsyish." Insofar as many Rom had to make do with what they could acquire as hand-me-downs, there is a great latitude in what you can wear and still pass as Gypsy. Study photographs. Check out the bibliography at the back of this book for other books on the Rom. The important thing, so far as working magic goes, is that you should *feel* you are dressed appropriately.

I will deal with magical tools in Chapter 15. The tool you will need depends on what you are trying to do. For now, let's start looking at some magical working.

5

BONDING AND BINDING:
Love, Lust, and Fascination

One of the most compelling forms of magic, and certainly the most sought after, is love magic. It is a positive form of magic and a way to true delight and pleasure. In my book *Secrets of Gypsy Love Magick* (St. Paul: Llewellyn, 1990) I broke down the subject into three sections: for courting; for newlyweds; and for the family unit. Although that is a convenient breakdown, I will not be using that division in this book. Rather, here I am presenting a broader variety of magic pertaining to love for you to use for whichever situation you feel it is best suited. Something that might be good in a courting situation could be equally useful for a newlywed, and vice versa.

A LOVE KNOT SPELL

Knots have always been used magically in spells. They can be employed in all aspects of love, whether in courtship, with the newly married, or f the love of family many years after marriage. In *Secrets of Gyp~   qic* I described the red ribbon with the seven knots in it, and   diklo. To illustrate how effective love knots can be, here is a   y:

Just nort'   he border between England and Scotland, Ivral Fergus ar   others and sisters spend the spring, summer, and fall. In th winter they all cross the border and head south, to spend the colder months in England's Sussex County. During their time in the north, the Ferguses travel back and forth on the Scottish side of the border, often within sight of the famous Hadrian's Wall, between Linton and Dumfries. It is said that a monstrous dragon once lived on Linton Hill, but it was eventually slain by the local hero. He fastened a wheel of burning peat to his lance and thrust it down the dragon's throat.

Ivral fell in love with her second cousin, Daniel Young, a handsome, brown-eyed young man who was teaching himself law and hoped, one day, to become one of the first Romany lawyers. Their families were happy with the match and everything seemed settled

44

when Daniel was offered a position with a Glasgow law firm. He would be little more than an office boy, he told Ivral, but it was a wonderful opportunity to be close to his subject and who knew where it might lead? She was happy for him but dreaded the coming long winter months without him, so "Old Liz," the *puridai* of the tribe, took Ivral aside and taught her the secret of the Love Knots.

The Romany society is an extremely chauvanistic one. The tribe is governed by a council of elders, who are all men. All the decisions, big and small, are made by these men: where to camp, who should work at what, when to move on and where, and, in many cases, who should marry whom. But there is one old woman—usually the grandmother, or great-grandmother of the family—who is greatly respected. She is known as the *puridai* (from *puri* "old" and *dai* "mother"). She is not necessarily a shuvani, though many times that is her role. (Just as often there is another person who is shuvani, or shuvano for the tribe.) The men make a big show of making decisions and directing others, but they always advise the puridai of their decision before announcing it to the rest of the tribe. If she nods her head when told, then the men go ahead and announce their decision. But if she says something like, "Hmm. You are certain that's your decision?" or "And you feel you've taken everything into consideration?" or some such remark, then the leader goes back to the other men and they rethink it! The final announced decision is always the one that the puridai has agreed is the right one. So, despite their facade, the men are very much living in a matriarchal society!

So it was, then, that Ivral was taken aside and given advice by this wisest of the wise of the tribe. What the puridai told her was this:

To be out of sight of the one you love is not the same as being out of his heart. He should be thinking of you night and day until he sees you again. To bring this about you need to tie his heart to yours. Take a personal item of clothing from him—a handkerchief or a diklo (neck scarf), or something similar. It should be something that he has used or worn many times. It can be washed, so that it is clean, but it should be something that he's used for a long time. The ideal item would be a piece cut from an undergarment, such as the tail of a shirt or undershirt. On this piece of cloth, mark his name and yours, enclosed in a heart.

In earlier times, the young woman would embroider the names and the heart, concentrating her thoughts on the two of them together through every stitch she made. Today, many young folk would use a felt-tip pen or similar writing tool. This will do (though if you really want to put as much power as possible into the charm, do it the old way!), but you must still concentrate on the two of you while writing. The names should be done in green and the heart in red.

Roll the cloth, lengthwise, into a tight, thin tube. Then tie it in a knot at the middle, and tie another knot at each end—three knots in all. As you tie the knot in the middle, say (aloud) his name and yours. As you tie the knot at one end, repeat your name. As you tie the knot at the other end, repeat his name.

Wear the knotted piece of cloth against your skin for three days and nights. This you can do by tucking it into your underclothes and, at night, beneath your nightdress or pajamas. At the end of that time, give it to your lover, with a kiss. He must always keep it on his person and then he will never forget you. You will be in his thoughts constantly.

Ivral did this charm and gave the cloth to Daniel. He placed it in his *putsi* (Gypsy pouch), which he wore on a cord around his neck, under his shirt, at all times. When Ivral returned to Scotland in the spring, Daniel welcomed her back with open arms and swore his love for her anew.

A Gypsy's *putsi* or pouch might be similar to these.

This spell can be done in any situation similar to Ivral's and Daniel's. It can also be done between husband and wife, mother and son, or any other combination of loved ones where there is a desire to remain in each other's thoughts while apart. Many times two such knotted cloths are prepared and given, one from the woman to the man and another from the man to the woman.

Finding a natural knot is especially powerful love magic. To find a vine that has grown into a knot, or willow twigs that have done the same, is extremely lucky. Gypsies in some areas believe that the spirits, or fairies, have tied these knots. If a man can find such a knot and place it in the bed (under the mattress?) of the woman he loves, they will become as one, so goes the old belief. It will, of course, work the other way around, with a woman placing it in the bed of a man.

HAIR CHARMS

Another powerful tool for bringing two people together, or keeping them together, is to take a lock of hair from each of them. The hair should be cut in the waxing cycle of the moon. Tie the locks together in one love-lock with red silk thread or ribbon. Again, picture the two people joyfully together while tying the knot, and as you tie it, say:

> *Kay o kám, avriável,*
> *Kiya mánge lele beshel*
> *Kay o kám tel' ável,*
> *Kiya lelákri me beshav.*

> Where the sun goes up
> Shall my love be by me.
> Where the sun goes down
> There by her I'll be.

Then wear the hair in a locket above the heart. This is a Hungarian Gypsy charm.

Charles Leland (*Gypsy Sorcery,* 1891) says that in the Tyrol, horses' manes that have become tangled and twisted by the Chagrin, a mischievous demon, must not be cut off or disentangled unless the words *Cin tu jid', cin ádá bálá jiden* ("So long live thou, long as these hairs shall live") are spoken. He goes on to say that in Europe knots in the hair are believed made by witches and should not be disentangled for fear of loosing some spell. The Gypsies do believe that shuvanis can lock up luck—good or bad—in knots, and knots in hair are always suspect.

It is said that if you sleep with your lover and, without his or her knowledge, you tie a knot in his hair, he will be unable to get you out of his mind.

If a woman can creep up, unseen, on a sleeping man and snip off a lock of his hair without waking him, she will hold his affections for as long as she carries the hair with her. However, if she does wake him while doing this, or is seen by anyone else, he will despise her!

To end a love affair, cut a lock from your lover's hair without his or her knowledge, and burn it in the light of a new moon. Before the next new moon you will go your separate ways.

New Forest Gypsies wear a charm made from hair taken from the mane or tail of a wild pony. The pony must be piebald or skewbald. The hair is plaited into a ring and worn as a bracelet for luck. Spanish Gypsies favor the tail hair from a black mare. They will thread various charms onto the finished length of plaited hair.

YOUR PROSPECTIVE MATE

There are several ways to find out who or what type of person you will marry. One—from the old days of *jallin' a drom*, or "traveling the road"—was for the woman to take the seeds of an apple she had eaten and mix them into some dampened earth taken from under where her vardo or bender had stood the previous night. She should then spread the earth and seeds in the middle of a crossroads. If a man is the first to pass over the seeds, then she will marry a young bachelor. If it's a woman who first passes over them, then she will marry an older man, one who may have been married before.

Another apple divination: You must obtain an apple from a widow without thanking her for it. Eat half of the apple before midnight and the other half after midnight. You will then dream of your future spouse. One group of Gypsies says that this must be done on St. Andrew's Eve (the night of November 29, although many Gypsies adhere to the Old Style calendar and celebrate the Eve on December 10). Others say it must be done on the night of the full moon. Still other Gypsies say it really doesn't matter when you do it!

If you are trying to choose between several equally appealing people as a mate, try using the Gypsy pendulum. Write the names of potential mates on a sheet of paper, with the names going out from the center like a star (as shown here). Make sure that no name is directly opposite another. Then, go to the woods and find an acorn. Tie the acorn on the end of a nine-inch length of red silk thread and hold the end of the thread so that the acorn hangs down, like a pendulum. Sit with it suspended over the center of the paper, just off the surface. Say aloud each of the names written on the paper. Then, clearing your mind of them, concentrate on having the ideal mate. The pendulum will start to swing backwards and forwards. It will swing along the line of one of the names. This is the one who is right for you. If it should swing exactly between two names, then write just those two names on another piece of paper, one horizontally and the other vertically, and try again. It will then swing along one name only.

Gypsy shuvanis often use pendulums, especially for determining health problems. Many times they have made one which they keep tucked into their putsi, or hanging around their neck. They will carve a piece of wood, or bone, and fasten it to a length of cord. The wood is decorated with magical symbols (see Chapter 15).

Another old Gypsy way of deciding between suitors is to write each name on a slip of paper and roll the slip into a ball of clay. The balls are dropped into a cauldron of spring water. The piece of paper that rises to the surface first carries the name of the true love.

Gypsies in Transylvania believe that divining one's future spouse must be done on the eve of the New Year. At that time you throw an old shoe up into a willow tree. If it catches on a branch—even if it falls down again after a moment—then it means you will be married in that coming year.

German Gypsies say to scratch the letters of the alphabet in the dirt. They don't have to be in a straight line; in fact it's better if they're not. Just scratch them, in no particular order and with a generous space between each, over an area roughly circular. Then take two horseshoes and walk nine paces away from the letters. Turn your back on them and pitch the horseshoes, one after the other, over your shoulder at the group of letters. The two letters you hit are the initials of the one who is to be your mate. If only one horseshoe hits a letter, and the other falls outside the area, then you have only one initial to go on, which could be for a first name or a last. If both horseshoes fall outside the area, you may try again. You can have up to three tries. If the shoes still do not fall on any of the letters, you will not marry that year.

In the area along the border between France and Belgium I came across a family of Gypsies. One of the *raklies* (young girls) told me of a charm she had learned from her grandmother, for seeing the face of the one you will marry. I have since come across this same charm in rural Missouri. Hard-boil an egg, cut through the white, and remove the yolk. Roll the yolk liberally in salt, and then replace it inside the white. Just before going to bed, eat the salted egg. During the night, I was assured, you will dream that you need a drink of water and someone will bring water to you in a water carrier. You will clearly see the face of the person and it will be the face of the one you will marry.

DRAWING HIM OR HER TO YOU

Sometimes the one you desire doesn't seem to know that you exist. Here is a spell told to be by an old shuvano named Plato Sheen, in the *Nevi Wesh* (the New Forest) in England. Plato was what is known as a "black blood" (*kaulo ratti*); that is a pure blood Romany. He assured me that this spell always works!

Find thirteen white stones. You may get them anywhere, but it's best if you go for a walk and can find them all as you walk. However, if necessary you may gather them over a period of time, picking up white stones you see until you eventually have thirteen. On the first Friday after a new moon, lay out the stones on the ground in the shape of a heart. Then lie flat on the ground, over the stones, so that your heart is over this heart of stones. Close your eyes and concentrate your thoughts on the one you want to notice you. Think of everything about him or her: physical appearance, interests, job, and so on. Then sit up and rearrange the stones into his or her initials.

Again lie down with your heart over the stones. This time, concentrate your thoughts on yourself: your looks, interests, feelings, especially your interest in this person. After you have done this for a while, gather up the stones and tie them up in a piece of white cloth. Carry this bundle with you until the full moon. By that time the person will have noticed you.

Let me make a point here: *Do not concentrate your thoughts on having him or her fall in love with you.* That would be too much of an enforcement of your will over theirs. As it is, perhaps this is a gray area, but the purpose is simply to cause them to *notice* you. If they do that, then if they're to fall in love with you they will. If it's not meant to be, they won't. As the old saying goes, let nature take its course.

A beautiful young Gypsy in Hampshire told me that if she wanted to dream of one of her boyfriends, she would write the names of all of them (she had seven!) on a piece of paper. When she went to bed she would tuck the folded paper between her breasts. Unfailingly she would dream of one of them and she paid special attention to which one it was. She said that when she dreamed of the same one three nights in a row, using this method, she felt certain he would be the one she would end up marrying.

Another young Gypsy in Devon told me that the best way to bring someone to you, or to get them to become interested in you, is to obtain something belonging to that person. It could be a piece of cloth, a glove, a shoe, a letter or other sample of handwriting, even a coin that they have possessed for a long time (so that it has absorbed their energy, presumably). Take that object and, if it's possible—as with the cloth, glove or shoe—fill it with the herb rue. If it's not something that can be filled, then place it—the coin, or whatever (in the case of a letter or other paper, fold it carefully three times)—in a white cloth bag filled with rue. In other words, depending on the object it is either filled with rue itself, or it is buried/concealed in rue. Then the rue-filled container should be hung from the corner of your bed, from the new moon until the full moon. By the end of that time the person will have contacted you.

An unusual spell comes from the North Yorkshire area of England. It is to conjure up the specter of your future spouse and make it appear. Several girls will sit around a campfire, away from the rest of the tribe. They will keep quiet and each will carefully roll a lock of her hair and some fingernail clippings in a green leaf. This they will place in the embers at the edge of the dying fire. If they keep quiet and concentrate, it is said that they will each see their future husband, in ghostly form, come forward and move the leaf to save it from burning.

LOVE CHARMS

Pierre Derlon (*Secrets of the Gypsies*, 1977) mentions a charm that I have found in many parts of England as well as in France. Derlon suggests it is used for friendship between a man and a woman, but I have found it used for cementing love rather than simple friendship.

It is used when a *juvvel* and a *mush* (Gypsy woman and man) belong to two different tribes, or two different branches of the same family. Perhaps they come together when the tribe meets for the long winter months. Or perhaps they meet once a year at the big horse fair, and the rest of the year are apart. When they first meet and fall in love, the juvvel promises she will find the root of a wild dog rose before the next time they come together. They part and go their separate ways. Then, every night that the mush has his vardo parked away from her, he will take a handful of earth from under its wheels and place it in a sack. He must hold up the sack, off the ground, while he places the soil in it. He puts just one handful in it each night, but slowly and surely the sack begins to fill as the days go by. By the time the year has run its course and they meet again, he has a full sack of earth. He gives it to the juvvel and she plants the wild dog rose in it. This becomes a symbol of their union and their desire to be together. As the rose grows and blossoms forth, so will their love grow and bloom.

If a woman falls in love with a married man, she must give him a white stone that she has taken from a running stream. She must first carry the stone in a small, white silk bag, between her breasts for a full cycle of the moon. Then she gives it to him at the new moon. If he carries this stone with him for a full month (another cycle of the moon), his wife will leave him and the woman will become his new lover.

6

HEALTH AND HEALING:
Physical Maintenance

The Gypsy witches, the shuvanis and shuvanos, are excellent healers. For centuries the Gypsies have been able to look after their own health very successfully. The Rom will not go to a gaujo doctor unless absolutely necessary. They don't trust them—one of the Rom words for doctor is *mullomengro,* which means "dead man maker" or "ghost maker."

The shuvani has an excellent knowledge of herbs, of course, and these are used primarily for health and healing. The chapter "Herbalism" in my book *Buckland's Complete Book of Witchcraft* (St. Paul: Llewellyn, 1986) could as well have been placed in this present book, for the Wiccan and Gypsy thoughts and knowledge on herbal lore are very much the same, but the Rom will frequently accompany their use of herbs with magical chants and spells. Richard Lucas (*Common and Uncommon Uses of Herbs for Healthful Living,* New York: Prentice-Hall, 1969) speaks of "the remarkable knowledge of herbal remedies that the Gypsies possessed. Their caravans can be seen loaded with mysterious boxes of freshly gathered herbs as the roaming Gypsies travel from village to village, selling their aromatic merchandise, and relating to the villagers the herbal folklore that dates from the misty regions of the past."

In this chapter are some of the more popular Gypsy herbal cures, along with the magical aspects of using them. Let me start at the top of the body and work down. [*Publisher's Note: Some remedies described here involve substances or methods which may not be safely used. This is not a medical book, but is a report of cultural or historical practices.*]

HEAD AND NECK PROBLEMS

Baldness and Thinning Hair
Rosemary (*Rosemarinus officinalis*) is very good for promoting hair growth. Gypsies will boil an ounce of dried rosemary in a pint of

water and keep it on the boil for 5 minutes. When cool, rub the liquid into the scalp. This should be done in the light of the moon, and it should be in the waxing phase of the moon, not the waning phase. As you rub in the liquid, say the following three times:

> *Te del amen o gulo*
> *Del eg meschibo pa amara choribo*

This is from Transylvanian Gypsies and, so far as I can translate, means: "May the sweet God give us a remedy for our poverty."

A remedy for baldness, from some French Gypsies, is to thoroughly mix a dram (1.771 grams) of Chrysarobin (or "goa" powder, the pith found in the wood *Andira araroba*) in 2 ounces of pure hog lard. The resulting mixture should be well rubbed into the scalp. Do this every day and new hair will grow, I've been assured.

To stop hair loss, say some Gypsies in the southwest of England, make a mixture of tallow and wild cherry bark, together with some scrapings from an old piece of harness (preferably the bridle). This can be rubbed into the hair as a restorer. To have a heavy growth of hair, with your left hand you must scoop up water from a running stream, against the current, and pour it on your head.

A cure for dandruff is to wash your hair in a tea made from peach tree leaves to which a little sulphur has been added. Another cure is to wash it in a tea made from wild cherry bark or one made from sage. The latter will also restore the color to graying hair.

Nearly all Gypsies seem to follow the belief that to cut your hair in the waning of the moon will keep it short far longer than cutting it in the waxing phase. The increase of the moon seems to promote increase in hair growth.

Headaches

There are many Romany cures for headaches; all of them are good. In Essex county, England, Gypsies told me to rub the head as hard as you can with warm water to which apple cider vinegar has been added. As you rub the head you must chant:

> Oh, pain in my head,
> The father of all evil
> Look upon me now!
> Thou hast greatly pained me.
> Remain not in me!
> Go thou, go thou, go home,
> Home to the Devil.
> Thither, thither hasten!
> Who treads upon my shadow,
> To him be the pain!

The last two lines above are reminiscent of the old charm for getting rid of a sty in the eye:

> Sty! Sty! Leave my eye!
> Catch the one who's passing by!

Another headache charm is simply to tie a length of blue wool around the head and wear it until the headache goes away...which it will. Some people will put a band of blue cloth around the inside of their hat.

Welsh Gypsies concoct a tonic for headaches using willow bark (*Salix alba*) and St. John's Wort (*Hypericum perforatum*). They say to pulverize the willow bark and chop the St. John's Wort into tiny pieces. You put 6 teaspoons of the bark and ¾ teaspoon of the St. John's Wort into a kettle (be sure it's not aluminum) and cover with about four cups of water. Simmer for about 15 minutes, then let it stand and cool. Strain it off and you will have enough for taking three or four cups of the tonic throughout the day.

On the purely magical side, a headache can be charmed away by placing a lock of your hair underneath a stone, turning your back on it and walking quickly away, saying: *Sherro shookar* nine times, in time with your first nine paces.

Scottish Gypsies say to rid yourself of a headache, boil an ounce of Ladies' Slipper root (*Cypripedium pubesceno*) in a pint of water. Boil it for 10 minutes, then let it cool. Strain, and take a wineglassful once each hour.

Eye Problems

For red, inflamed eyes, Gypsy Petulengro, an English Gypsy well known in the 1930s, suggested taking enough Bluestone to cover a sixpence (an old English coin about the size of a dime) and placing it in an eight-ounce bottle. Fill the bottle with water that has been boiled, and shake until the Bluestone has dissolved. Use this as an ordinary eyewash after the water has completely cooled. The water can come off the boil when it is added but should still be warm enough to dissolve the Bluestone.

My grandmother used an old Buckland Gypsy recipe: simmer a tea-spoon of fennel seed (*Foeniculum officinale*) in a cup of water until the liquid turns a golden color. Remove from the heat and allow to cool. Strain. The resulting liquid made an eye wash my grandmother considered a great cure for sore and tired eyes.

An old Welsh recipe for inflamed eyelids called for: ¼ ounce of red mercuric oxide, 1 ounce of purified coconut oil, and ¾ ounce of pure lard, mixed together thoroughly and spread on the eyelids. [Not recommended—mercuric oxide is classified as a poison.—Ed.]

The weed eyebright (*Euphrasia officinalis*), as you might guess from its old folk name, is excellent for eye problems. Saffron (*Carthamus tintorius*) is also used. It is steeped in spring water or well water and used as an eye wash. While using it, you must say:

> Oh, pain from the eyes go into the water,
> Go into the water, into the herb,
> Into the earth. To the Earth Spirit.
> There is your home; there go and feast.

Another common plant used for eye problems was elder blossom (*Sambu cus Canadensis*). This is used by Gypsies around the world.

In fact, according to Lucas, they refer to the elder as "the healingest tree on earth." It certainly can be used in the curing of coughs and colds and for making various healing ointments. For eyes, a wash is made by steeping elder flowers in water and then bathing the eyes. Similarly, wormwood (*Artemisia absinthium*) tea is excellent as an eye wash.

It is not uncommon, when traveling the dusty back roads, for a Gypsy to get something in his eye. The Rom remedy for this is to drop 2 drops of warm olive oil directly onto the eyeball.

An interesting charm, used by some Gypsies both in southeast England and in France and Belgium, is to cut hair from the tail of a black cat and place it in a small green silk bag. The bag is then rubbed across the eye(s) with the words *Shoon, dick, ta rig dre zi.* This is good for all eye problems, even cataracts, I've been told.

Ear Problems

An old remedy for earache, used by Gypsies and gaujos alike, is to fill a small bag with salt, warm it by the fire, or in the oven (be careful not to get it too hot), then place it on the ear or lie down with the ear resting on the bag.

A Rom remedy for both earache and headache is to hold a white bone button in the mouth, under the tongue.

Many Gypsies, if they have any sort of ear trouble, will take the fresh plant extract from the broad-leaved plantain (*Plantago major*), and continue taking it for several weeks if necessary. Some Gypsies, however, swear by a mixture of rosemary (*Rosmarinus officinalis*), wood betony (*Betonica officinalis*), wood sage (*Teucrium Canadensis*), mistletoe (*Viscum album*), and shepherd's purse (*Capsella bursa-pastoris*). These ingredients are mixed in equal parts, then two teaspoons are placed in a teacup and boiling water is poured over them. This is allowed to stand for five minutes before drinking. Gypsies in Cornwall always add a little honey and milk to it, which certainly makes it more palatable.

The *hotchi-witchi*, the European hedgehog, is much enjoyed by the Rom. It is a tasty delicacy but it also has healing qualities. When disemboweling a hedgehog, you will find a blue-green bag-like gland containing oil that is excellent for treating earache.

Toothache

A cure for the toothache is to carry, or wear in a bag around the neck, the paw of a hedgehog. If the toothache is really bad, then it pays (apparently) to suck on the paw from time to time. Another common, if temporary, cure for toothache is to place a teabag between the tooth and the inner lip. In the days before the general proliferation of tea bags, Gypsies would make a little bag of tea-filled muslin for this purpose.

An old Welsh Gypsy told me that as a child suffering from toothache, he was taken into the woods by his uncle and made to stand with his back against a tree (he thinks it was a cedar tree). His uncle then hammered a horseshoe nail into the tree at the height of the aching tooth. He recalls that almost immediately the toothache went away and never came back.

A cure used by many Rom is to wear a special small pouch (*putsi*) around the neck. The pouch contains a horse's tooth. This is also used to make a baby's teething easier. The putsi, in that case, is often placed under the pillow in the baby's bed. Another way to ease teething is to hang a silver coin on a silver chain around the baby's neck.

Charles Leland (*Gypsy Sorcery*, 1891) reports that Transylvanian Gypsies cure a toothache by tying a barley straw around a stone and throwing the stone into a running stream, with the words:

> Oh, pain in my teeth trouble me
>   not so greatly!
> Do not come to me, my mouth is not
>   thy house.
> I love thee not at all; stay away from me.
> When this straw is in the brook, go away
>   into the water.

Another charm against toothache is found in the north of England. It is simply to say:

> Peter was sitting on a marble stone
> And Jesus passed by.
> Peter said, "My Lord, my God,
> How my tooth doth ache!"
> Jesus said, "Peter art whole!
> And whosoever keeps these words for My sake
> Shall never have the toothache."

Also in the north of England there is an old Gypsy tradition for getting rid of a toothache: The sufferer would carry a red flannel bag filled with a piece of coal, a crust of bread, and a pinch of salt. Interestingly enough, these are the same three ingredients that the Scottish "first footer" (the first person to enter the house on the first day of the new year) must carry when stepping over the threshold, in order to bring prosperity to the house in the coming months.

Complexion

A "complexion improver" is made from the goa powder mentioned earlier in connection with baldness. This is Chrysarobin, a yellowish powder found in tree trunks in Brazil that was very popular with European healers. It was used for all sorts of skin diseases because of its chrysophanic acid content. For a facial, mix the goa powder with vinegar, lemon juice, or glycerine to form a paste, and apply to the skin.

For acne, a tea is made from common yarrow blossoms (*Achillea millefolium*) and wild teasel roots (*Dipsacus sylvestris*). The Gypsies say that the teasel should be gathered right after the first full moon of the fall and air-dried in a shady spot. Place the teasel in a container (about a handful of it) and cover with a quart of cold water. Bring to a boil and keep just on the boil for about ten minutes, then remove from the heat. In a separate container, put a handful of the yarrow blossoms and pour the hot teasel over them. Cover the pot and let it sit for fifteen minutes before straining. Twice a day, sip a cup of this tea. Just after rising and just before going to bed are good times to drink it.

Many Gypsy women believe that the very best facial they can get is fresh semen from a handsome Rom! (The favored methods for procuring this were not shared with me.) However, one precaution mentioned was to keep the semen from getting into the eyes.

Applying fresh dew from the grass and also bathing the face in buttermilk are age-old remedies for rough skin and/or pimples. Many young Gypsy girls, the *raklies*, will cover their faces with the skin pared off a cucumber. A tea made from sassafras (*Sassafras varifolium*) is another good aid to complexion.

Mud packs may be favored by some women but Gypsy women don't hesitate to use a mixture of mud and cow dung! It is said to do a wonderful job. Another popular aid is water taken from the bucket in which a blacksmith has been tempering horseshoes.

Petulengro gives a recipe for a beauty ointment: 2½ ounces Spermaceti, ½ pint almond oil, 1 ounce white wax (or lanolin; coconut oil is also softer and easier to work with), ¼ ounce benzoin (coarse powder), ½ ounce prepared calamine. All of these are melted together over a gentle heat, then strained through a very fine sieve. The resulting ointment is then kept in airtight jars. It can be used freely at night, before going to bed, or sparingly in the daytime.

Another good Gypsy beauty cream is made from 1 ounce red dock root, 2 ounces elder tree flowers, 2 ounces cold cream, and 2 ounces pure pork lard. The dock root is cut up and, with the elder tree flowers, added to the lard in an earthen jar. It is heated, on a low heat, for an hour to an hour and a half. The mixture is then strained and the cold cream added. They are mixed together until cold. This is a good general face cleanser and purifier, especially effective against blackheads.

Nose and Throat Complaints

For a nosebleed, Charles Leland (*Gypsy Sorcery*, 1891) gives a strange-sounding spell (used not only for nosebleeds but to stop any form of excessive bleeding). It is to say the following:

Dumb sat on a hill
With a dumb child in arms.
Dumb the hill was called;
Dumb was called the child.
The holy Dumb
Heal (bless) this wound!

The whole spell sounds somewhat dumb, but it was effective enough that it has been used for generations. How or why it would work, I could not attempt to guess.

Another Rom charm to stop bleeding, especially a nosebleed, is to face the east and, raising both arms, cry out the name of the afflicted person and the words "Stop, blood! Stop!"

Gypsies in Devon and Cornwall say you must cry: "Three roses in Gana's name! Stop, blood! Stop!"

While on the subject of bleeding, Irene Soper says that the Manouche Gypsies of Alsace-Loraine apply crushed puffball fungi to a wound to stop the bleeding and help heal the wound.

One of the best cures for a sore throat is a tea made from Healall (*Prunella vulgaris*). Use one ounce of the herb to one pint of water. Take a wineglassful of the tea (warm or cold) three times a day. This is very effective.

Gypsies in the New Forest make what they call sloe syrup for sore throats. Ripe sloes are cleaned off the stalks and leaves and then placed in layers, alternating with sugar, in a canning jar. The jar is filled in this way, building up the layers one on top of the other. The lid is put on when the jar is full, and it is put away, out of the light, for at least three weeks. At the end of that time, the sloes have shriveled up and dropped to the bottom of the jar. The syrup should be drained off and kept in a separate container. Administer by the teaspoonful for a sore throat. (Sloes are the tart, plum-like fruit of the blackthorn shrub.)

To cure, or ward off, tonsillitis, Gypsy children wear an antique gold coin around their neck. Victorian sovereigns and half-sovereigns are popular for this. Today (1998) a gold sovereign is worth between $400 and $500.

CHEST AILMENTS

Asthma

A Spanish Gypsy's treatment for bronchial asthma is to make a tea of coltsfoot leaves (*Tussilago farfara*), lavender blossoms (*Lavandula officinalis*), lungwort (*Pulonaria officinalis*), and mallow blossoms (*Althea officinalis*). You mix together equal parts of the four herbs, then make a tea using a tablespoonful of the mix to a pint of water. Let it steep for a quarter of an hour. This tea should be drunk four times a day. Some people sweeten it with honey, but if you can manage without that it's better.

Many Gypsies dry the berries of the sumac (*Rhus glabra*) and smoke them in a pipe to cure asthma. Berries picked in late fall are best. They should be spread out in a very thin layer, on a piece of canvas, and left exposed to the air. Then they are heated, on a low heat, in an oven. Finally they are again spread out on canvas and left for 24 hours. Some say that this is better for smoking than the finest tobacco. Some Gypsies dry the leaves, also, and use them. Others mix either the dried berries or leaves with regular tobacco.

A cure for asthma is to catch a trout, breathe deeply into its mouth three times, and then throw it back into the river.

For the relief of asthma, many Gypsies recommend drying the leaves of nettles (*Urtica dioica*) and then burning them and inhaling the smoke. An old Welsh Gypsy assured me that to prevent or even cure asthma you needed to take the dried skin of a mole and stick it to your chest with honey.

For asthma and other chest complaints, Petulengro suggests boiling an ounce of sweet chestnut tree leaves (*Castanea vesca*) in 1½ pints of water. Boil for 10 minutes, then strain and allow to cool. Add ½ ounce of honey and ½ ounce of glycerine. Take a wineglassful when you first get up in the morning and then another in the evening after your last meal of the day.

Breast Cancer
Gypsy women will wear the foot of a mole, hanging on a green thread, ribbon, or length of wool between their breasts, to keep them free of breast cancer.

Common Cold
There is a New Forest Gypsy recipe for elder syrup that was considered very effective against the common cold. Gather elderberries and place 2 or 3 quarts in a stone jar and cover them with a plate. Put the jar into a pan of boiling water and keep it there until the juice starts to flow from the berries. Then turn out the berries into a piece of muslin and squeeze them. Put the resulting juice in a pan with 1 pound of sugar for each quart of juice. Add a few cloves and bring to a boil. Take the syrup off the heat and allow it to cool before bottling it in a number of small, corked, bottles. It should be kept in a cool place. One teaspoonful 3 times a day is the usual dosage.

Heartburn
An old English cure for heartburn (not just Gypsy) is to make a tea of blackberry leaves, long-spurred pansy roots, oak bark, rose leaves, and sage leaves. Mix well together 1 handful of the blackberry leaves with 2 handsful of each of the other ingredients. Store in an airtight jar. To make the tea, take a tablespoonful of the mix for each cup of water. Pour the boiling water over the mix, cover, and let steep for a quarter hour. Strain and let cool. Drink one cup of the cold tea, sipping it 3 times a day.

STOMACH PROBLEMS

Stomachache
A Gypsy I met in Florida told me of a charm used by his people in his native Hungary. If one of the small children has stomach pains they will burn the hairs of a black dog. The mother's milk and some of the

child's feces are mixed with the resulting ashes or powder to form a paste. The paste is put into a cloth and bound to the child's stomach. The child sleeps with this poultice; at sunrise the poultice is taken off and carried into the woods. There a hole is bored in the trunk of a tree and the paste-filled cloth is stuffed into the hole. The hole is then plugged up with a wooden plug, and the following words are said by the shuvani or the mother:

> Depart from the belly
> And live in the tree!
> Remain, remain here,
> I say to thee!

In the southwest of England, Gypsies will finely chop the gizzard of a chicken and make a tea from it. This, they say, is a wonderful cure for stomach cramps and any sort of stomach-ache. In that same area, a cure for gastritis is to boil an ounce of oak bark in a quart of water and keep it on the boil until the liquid becomes a fine golden color, then remove it from the heat and let it cool. One wineglassful of the liquid can be taken after each meal.

Bladder Problems

Parsley mint (*Alchemilla arvensis*) is good for bladder problems. Simply boil an ounce of parsley mint in a pint of water for about a minute. Let it cool, strain it, and drink a wineglassful twice a day. Gravel Root, or Queen of the Meadow (*Eupatorium purpureum*), is also good for bladder problems when made into a strong tea, which can later be diluted. Try a tablespoon in a quart of water, boiling it for 5 minutes. Couch grass root (*Agropyrum repens*) is similarly good. Boil an ounce of this in 1 cup of water for 5 minutes. As above, let it cool, strain it, and drink a wineglassful 6 times a day.

In many Gypsy tribes (as is also found in parts of the Ozarks) frequent sexual intercourse is looked upon as an excellent cure for bladder and kidney problems in women!

Hemorrhoids

A traditional Gypsy ointment for treating hemorrhoids is made from leaves of the plantain (*Plantago major*) and of ground ivy (*Nepeta glechoma*), together with pure lard. Take 4 ounces of the lard, 1 ounce of the plantain, and ½ ounce of the ground ivy. Boil them together over low heat for about 10 minutes. The leaves should be well pressed into the lard to extract their goodness, then it should be strained into a jar and left to cool. To protect yourself from getting hemorrhoids, always carry a horse-chestnut (*Aesculus hippocastanum*) or a buckeye (*Aesculus glabra*) in your pocket or purse.

ARMS AND LEGS

Rheumatism and Arthritis

There are many Gypsy remedies for rheumatism and arthritis. Probably the simplest is to stew a few celery sticks—preferably with the leaves on—in a little milk, then to eat them and drink the liquid. This should be done daily for at least a week. Continuous drinking of lentil juice (from lentils soaked in water) is considered a great preventive. One Gypsy family claims that carrying a walnut keeps them free of rheumatism. Another says it should be a nutmeg. Many Gypsies favor wearing copper bracelets for this. Dandelion root (*Taraxacum officinale*) is another commonly available ingredient for rheumatism. Boil an ounce of the root in 1½ pints of water for 20 minutes. Strain and cool. Drink a wineglassful of this tea twice a day.

Many English Gypsies believe that binding the skin of a snake, or an eel, around the joint will ease rheumatic and arthritic pain. Some say that just to carry the skin with you is efficacious. This is also good for any stiff joints, a swollen knee, tennis elbow, and the like. Slavic Gypsies will stick wood chips into an egg. They then wrap it up and hang it somewhere in the vardo. As the egg gradually shrinks, so will the swelling, they say.

A treatment for lumbago that is used in most Gypsy tribes is to extract the oil from juniper berries (*Juniperus communis*) and rub that into the affected area.

Warts

There are many ways to charm away warts. The old Buckland Gypsy method is to rub the wart with the cut side of half a potato. As you rub it you say:

So must mandi ker 'te ker tutti mishto?
Lel a-drom waffedi; latcher sasti.

What must I do, to make you well?
Take away badness; find wellness.

You then take the half-potato and bury it, cut side up, at least six inches in the ground. As the potato rots, so will the wart gradually disappear. I have used this numerous times, very successfully. A similar method is for the shuvani to tie a string around the wart and say those same words. Then the string is pulled off and the "wart bearer" is told to bury it where no one will find it. In nine days the wart will be gone.

Many people will spit on the wart and then rub it with a small piece of paper. The paper is then dropped at a crossroads and the first person to pass over it inherits the wart. There is another belief that if you rub the wart with a piece of bacon rind and then nail the rind to a tree, the wart will slowly disappear. New Forest Gypsies told me to find a small stone that looked like the wart, rub that on the actual wart, and then throw it into a moving stream.

Wild garlic juice is good for wart removal. Simply dab it onto the wart 9 times, in the light of the full moon, then let the moonlight fall on the wart for 3 minutes. A Spanish Gypsy says that during those 3 minutes you must think of the wart having gone and say:

Nasty wart, go away!
Part from me and do not stay.
Nasty wart, go away!

Greek Gypsies swear by the white liquid, or "milk," that issues from broken leaves and branches of the fig tree. Simply rub that milk onto the wart and it will disappear. Similarly, the white milk from the dandelion is effective. The end of a dandelion stalk can be touched to the wart, depositing the milk. It is then left to dry. When repeated three or four times a day, the wart is said to darken, turn black, and fall off.

Diarrhea

For diarrhea, nothing is as effective as the elderberry. You can eat the dry berries, stew them, or mix them in with your cereal. Any way you take them, they are an excellent remedy against diarrhea. Another effective remedy for this is a tea made from the fleabane, or horse weed (*Erigeron Canadense*). Another cure is a tea made from steeping ragweed (*Ambrosia artemisiaefolia*) in cold water.

Constipation

At the opposite extreme, the inner bark of the white walnut, or butternut (*Juglans cinerea*), is an excellent laxative. Gypsies boil it down to a thick syrupy texture, add flour and roll it into pills. Many give the pills a coating of sugar to make them more palatable. Dandelions are also a mild laxative and are often put into salads by the Gypsies.

Chilblains

Chilblains can best be treated with a mixture of lemon juice and glycerine. Another remedy, told to me with great seriousness, is to rub fresh urine on the spot. Petulengro says to use the water in which parsnips have been boiled (without salt). To 2 pints of the water, mix in 1 tablespoonful of powdered alum, and stir well. Bathe the area of the chilblains for a good 20 minutes, then allow it to dry without rinsing.

Various Complaints

For menstrual irregularity, boil 2 ounces of blue cohosh root (*Caliphyllum thalictroides*) in 3 pints of water for 20 minutes. Strain and bottle. Take a wineglassful twice a day. For menstrual pain, Gypsies swear by parsley (*Petroselinum sativum*).

For bruises, boil down some pig's fat and add to it the blossoms of an elder tree (best taken when the sun is on them). Crush the blossoms slightly before you add them. When cool, rub on the bruised area. The mixture can be put in a pot for future use.

For the skin, nettles (*Urtica dioica*) are very useful. Make a tea with a handful of nettle leaves to a quart of water. Steep for about 10 minutes. Drink a cup 3 times a day. You can also take ¼ ounce of baker's yeast in 1 teaspoon of fresh nettle juice, 6 times a day.

For skin diseases such as dermatoses, eczema, herpes, acne, and boils, mix 2 ounces red clover flowers (*Trifolium pratense*), 1 ounce burdock root (*Arctium lappa*), 1 ounce blue flag root (*Iris versicolor*), ½ ounce sassafras bark (*Sassafras variifolium*). Put a quarter of the mixture into a pint of cold water, bring it to the boil and simmer for 20 minutes. When cold, strain. Take one wineglassful 3 times a day.

To get rid of the sharp pain of a burn, a shuvani will cup the burn with her hand and mutter the words:

> Two 'Gyptians came out of the east.
> One brought fire and t'other brought frost.
> Out fire! In frost!

When she removes her hand, they say, the pain has gone.

Petulengro gives a wonderful recipe for what he calls a "Tonic Stout." It is made up of 1 ounce nettles, 1 ounce hops, 8 ounces black malt, ¼ ounce black licorice, 2 medium-size potatoes, 2 ounces brown sugar, and 1 ounce yeast. First add the herbs, malt, and hops to 10 pints of water, boil, and then add the licorice and potatoes. The potatoes should be washed, but not peeled, and should be pricked with a fork. Gently simmer the mixture until you have reduced it down to about 8 pints (1 gallon). After straining, turn out into an earthenware container. Stir in the sugar and yeast. This sugar and yeast should have been mixed beforehand with a little of the liquor, cooled in a cup or jug. Stir in well. Stand in a warm place for 24 hours with a cloth over the pan. At the end of that time, skim off the yeast that has risen to the top and then bottle the liquid. Put the tops on lightly first, then tighten them down in 12 hours. If you want a ruby tint to the stout, add an apple. Petulengro also suggests throwing in a few rusty nails, for the iron! Let the bottles stand for a couple of days. Be careful not to shake the bottles when you pour out the beverage.

HANDS-ON HEALING

Most of the shuvanis and shuvanos are superb healers, not only working with herbs and spells, but also doing hands-on work. Some few other Rom are also good healers in this way, though most of them have been especially chosen and taught this by a shuvani.

Pierre Derlon, in his book *Secrets of the Gypsies* (1977), speaks of "palming" and gives one method of doing the Rom "Sun-Moon" healing, as used by Gypsies in France. I have found similar methods used throughout the British Isles. In this method, the Rom healer uses her hands to represent the Sun and the Moon as a microcosm. Her right hand is the Sun and her left the Moon (if right-handed—left-handers use the reverse). The right hand is held almost like a claw, sending out the Sun's rays to heal. The left hand is held flat, reflecting back the sun's light, as does the Moon. Basically, with the Healer standing on the Recipient's right side, the hands are moved over the body—the right hand on the front of the body and the left hand on the back—so that the healing rays are sent *through* the body, though this is actually the second half of the ritual. The first half starts with a drawing-off of negativity, and for this the hands are held normally.

The Recipient stands with feet shoulder-width apart and with eyes closed. Much as in many Wiccan forms of healing, both persons are naked, or *nangi*. The healing then starts with an attunement. Facing the Recipient, the Healer takes his or her hands and they both breathe deeply, attuning to one another. This is kept up for a few moments, then they hug and, as the Healer steps back, she places her hands on either side of the Recipient's temples. With light finger pressure she further attunes, then starts the "drawing off." This is taking away the negativity that is in the body.

The two hands are slowly drawn down the sides of the Recipient: down the sides of the face, the outsides of the arms, the hips, the legs, to the ground. There the Healer will shake her hands, shaking off the negativity that has been drawn off. Then the right hand only is brought down the Recipient's left side, but this time on the inside of the arm, with the palm against the body. At the hip, the hand is passed across the pubic area and on down the inside of the right leg. Again it is shaken. This is repeated with the Healer's left hand on the other side, crossing at the pubic area again to the left leg, and on down to the ground and shaken.

There are five sets of passes made altogether: one set with both hands down the outside, then three sets of right hand followed by left hand, down the inside and crossing over. Then a final set of passes down the outer sides of the recipient's body again with both hands together. Each pass is finished with the shaking-off of the negativity. A "set," of course, is one pass with the right hand and one pass with the left hand.

Again the Healer puts her hands on either side of the recipient's head and again attunes. Then she moves to stand close, on the right of the Recipient. The Healer now places her right hand, in the "claw" shape, on the forehead of the Recipient, with her left, "flat" hand against the back of the head. She now concentrates her healing energies down her arm, out through her fingers, and through the Recipient. The energies are reflected back by the left hand and, mentally, the Healer keeps this up, sensing the energy moving back and forth between her two hands. By experience, she knows how long to continue this. She will then move down to the neck and repeat the pulsation of energy there. From there she goes to the heart. Next the left breast is done and then the right breast. From there the hands are moved on down to the abdominal area and finally to the pubic area.

It can be seen that the healing energies are worked at points corresponding to most of the chakra centers. The first point corresponds to the third eye position, the sixth or seventh chakra (some teachings show the third eye as the sixth chakra and the crown as the seventh; some reverse that). The throat is, of course, the fifth chakra; the heart the fourth; the stomach (or solar plexus) the third; and the genital area covers the first and second. I believe that originally this correlation was important, and that they did indeed tie in with the chakras and the kundalini energy, but today most Gypsies don't even know what is meant by "chakra." They just know that these are the points where the healing is concentrated.

It should be pointed out that the breasts do not fit in with the chakras. This is true but there is a good indication that the Gypsies were again way ahead of their time. One of the most common problems with women these days is breast cancer or its potential. By including the mammary glands in the healing cycle, the Rom work toward a more complete healing than many other systems offer.

By talking with the Recipient prior to doing the healing, the Healer ascertains the area giving the problem and can then concentrate especially on that area. If necessary, she will go back and give a "double-dose," as it were, at that point. I have heard wonderful accounts of near-miraculous cures resulting from this Gypsy Sun-Moon form of hands-on healing, when it is administered by a powerful shuvani.

Other less elaborate hands-on healing is also done and many healers have their own little secret methods of working, but all seem to have a vast knowledge ranging from herbal lore, through charms and spells, to hands-on. It is no wonder that they seldom, if ever, go to visit the mullomengro!

A Bow Top Vardo.

7

WEALTH AND RICHES:
The Magical Acquisition of Wealth

On the face of it, Gypsies are not rich. Traveling around the country, constantly on the move, they are not able to use banks even if they feel inclined to. Actually, in these days of automated teller machines, where you are not totally tied to a local bank, it would be possible for the Rom to use the system, but they still have a distrust of it, so Gypsies carry their money with them. They usually carry it in the form of jewelry—gold coins ornamenting their dress; rings and bracelets on their hands; earrings in their ears. In this way, their wealth is readily available to them, yet is also serving a purpose.

Gold is considered almost essential for all Gypsies to own and wear. Gold earrings are especially necessary. Gold brings the blessings of wealth and works like a money magnet—when you have it, more is attracted to you. Silver is not used much for personal adornment, but is used on the travelers' horses.

It is rumored that some Gypsies bury their money in secret places that only they know. There is some evidence for this, though it would be much rarer today, with so few Rom still traveling the roads.

Gypsies don't seem to desire possessing large amounts of money just for the sake of having it, as is the case with so many gaujos. Yet non-Gypsies believe the Rom have ways of obtaining wealth, of bringing it magically, and frequently ask the shuvani how this can be done. There are many explanations given and many superstitions concerning it.

One such superstition is that if a red ant crawls on you, you will become rich within the year. If a red bird—or a bird with any amount of red in its plumage—should fly over your head, it is an indication of money. If it flies from your left to your right, it is money coming; if right to left, it is money leaving. Robins, cardinals, red-wing blackbirds, and the like are always studied closely.

78

Still believed in by most Gypsies is the old belief that when you first glimpse the new moon and you turn over a coin in your pocket it will bring wealth. You must turn the coin and then not look at the moon again. Further, it is always good luck to be touching a silver coin when you look at the moon. The moon ties in so much with silver that many money spells are done relating to the phases of the moon.

Another superstition is that if a woman has hairs on her breast, she will become a wealthy woman! If a man has red in his beard, he will never want for money.

Although the Rom do not encourage their chavvis to believe in the tooth fairy, there is a belief that to bury a wisdom tooth in a grave-yard will bring money within six months. Gypsies in Yorkshire say that to bury the jawbone of a fox at the foot of an oak tree will bring good fortune, and Welsh Gypsies think the same result will come from nailing a hedgehog hide to a willow tree.

When you are in desperate need of money for some emergency there is one way to draw it to you, according to old Zorka, a shuvano I met in Scotland. In the waxing cycle of the moon, go into the woods and find seven acorns, three white stones, and a segment of moss about the size of your hand. The moss should be carefully lifted from the stone, tree trunk, or wherever you find it, so that it is in one piece like a piece of cloth. Place the acorns and the stones in the cen-ter of the green moss side of the segment and fold in the sides so that it becomes like a small package or parcel. Wrap it around with string, or anything that will keep it closed. You can then wrap it in a piece of clean, white cloth if you wish. Place it under your pillow and go to bed at sundown. Sleep with it under your pillow until midnight, then wake up and take it outside. In the light of the moon, bury the pack-age at least three inches deep under a bramble bush (wild raspberry, blackberry, multiflora rose, or whatever—it should be a bush with thorns on it). Walk three times, clockwise, around the spot where you have buried it, saying:

> *Mi Dovvel opral, dick tule opré*
> *mande*

My God above, look down upon me.

Say it once during each circumambulation; three times in all. Money will come to you before the next full moon.

Some people say that you need money to make money. Certainly the idea of a little seed money as a "money magnet" seems to work well. A family of Boswells, moving around the eastern side of England—Essex, Suffolk, Norfolk, Cambridgeshire and Lincolnshire— seemed to me to be very affluent, for travelers. I asked the leader of the tribe, Stan Boswell, what his secret was. He wouldn't admit that there was any secret at first, but eventually he grudgingly admitted that his branch of the Boswells had always been relatively well off.

"It's thanks to m'dad's *purodad* (his father's grandfather—his own great-grandfather)," he said. "He seemed to know things. I was only a wee chavvi when I heard the story from m'puridai". Apparently his grandmother told him that her father had taken a single gold coin from each family of the tribe—each of the branches of Boswells who were traveling together—and had melted them down to form one gold nugget. That lump of gold he had buried in a graveyard, one particular night. Exactly where it was buried he wouldn't say. It was a secret passed on only to the head of the tribe—the Gypsy King. Once a year, as they passed that part of the country, the Boswell leader would visit the site and chant a spell over the buried gold. Again, he would not tell me what it was that was chanted.

"You can laugh if y'like," he said, his face serious. "But we've never wanted for anything for so long as I can remember."

A Gypsy family grows, with sons marrying and getting their own vardos to house their own families. So the tribe would grow—all the wagons traveling together housing branches of the same family. The oldest male, from whom the others had sprung, was what might be termed the "king" of that family or tribe. Many, if not most, Rom do not recognize the word "king," but some do and it's a good descriptive word for the leader. Sometimes a son and his family will break away from the rest of the tribe and go off, traveling alone. They usually do this with the father's blessing—though not always; sometimes it's the result of disagreement—and usually they are welcomed back should they decide to return to the fold. Sometimes separated parts of the same family just come together again at certain times of the year, perhaps to winter together. When the leader dies, his eldest son usually inherits the position and title. The "jewels" of a Gypsy King are (usually) a gold ring with a black stone in it and a walking-stick with a silver horse's head handle.

These days such traveling groups are very small—perhaps only three or four vehicles (motor homes, today). In the old times, up until World War II, you would see a dozen or more colorful wagons traveling together.

A modern Vickers' Vardo.

8

POWER AND LUCK:
Aids to Good Living

To have power over others is something many people desire. To be able to cause someone to make a decision that would be in your favor; to steer someone away from a course that you felt could only bring them ruin; to bring two people together whom you know are meant for one another; to turn negatives into positives—all these, and more, are things many of us would like to be capable of. Yet in white magic, as subscribed to by Wiccans and others, it is forbidden to interfere with another's free will. (I spoke of this in Chapter 4.) The Gypsies, however, do not hesitate to do whatever they feel is right, and the shuvanis are guided only by their personal thoughts and feelings.

Bringing pressure to bear on someone can be viewed as "gray magic"—in other words, it is neither good nor evil. What you are doing is getting someone to make a decision when they otherwise might take a very long time making up their mind. This was often of importance to the Rom. Constantly moving, as they were, it was frequently necessary to get a quick decision on something. They didn't necessarily try to influence what that decision was, but simply see that the decision be made.

One way to bring pressure to bear on a person, according to some New Forest Gypsies, was to obtain a picture of that person. This would be laid on the ground, on a patch of bare earth, in direct sunlight. The shuvani would kneel before the picture and concentrate thoughts on what decision had to be made. Then, in a low chant, she would say:

> *Kolliko; to-divvus; akno!*
> *Av, mi shookarengro,*
> *Mendi jal a drom;*
> *Mendi jal a drom.*

> Tomorrow; today; now!
> Come, my slow one,
> We travel the road;
> We travel the road.

She would then spit on the picture and, with the thumb of her right hand, rub the saliva around and around, clockwise. Finally she would turn the picture face-down in the dirt and throw more dirt on top of it to cover it. She would then stamp on it and walk away. The decision would be made within twenty-four hours.

Spitting seems to be a feature in a number of Gypsy spells. In the wonderful old movie *Golden Earrings* (with Marlene Deitrich and Ray Milland), the Deitrich character spits a number of times for luck or to accompany a particular action. Also, near the beginning of the movie, she offers prayers to "spirits of earth and water," then spits. (For this movie, Marlene Deitrich herself researched the Rom, living in a Gypsy camp for a while. For the film she designed her own authentic costume, overruling Hollywood wishes. Romany Murvyn Vye plays a part in the movie and also sings the title song.)

Yaksa (pronounced "Yak-sha") is the collective name of the spirits of field, forest, stream, etc., in Indian folklore. They are very ancient, pre-Vedic beings sometimes referred to as the Sacred Folk. A favorite haunt for yaksas was in the village tree—the main sacred tree of the community. Garlands were hung from its branches and tiny lamps, cakes, and other offerings were placed at its foot. Gypsies still revere trees and some still leave offerings beneath them.

Traditionally, if a Gypsy boy insists on marrying a gaujo girl, she may be allowed to join the tribe—if the leaders agree to it, although she is forever treated as an outsider and never as a close family member. But if a Gypsy girl marries a gaujo boy, she has to leave the tribe to live with him; he is never accepted in. A Rom family in Shropshire was therefore greatly agitated when the beautiful niece of the family patriarch fell in love with a gaujo. Many of her cousins and second cousins were madly in love with her and deeply resented the "intrusion" of this outsider. No one wanted to lose her from the family.

The puridai (the family matriarch) felt that, for the good of everyone, action needed to be taken. The girl had been spoken to by many of the tribe's elders but seemed determined to go with her gaujo. The trick, then, decided the puridai, was to make the boy lose interest in her. It would hurt her for a while, but she would get over it, it was felt. Somehow someone obtained a lock of the boy's hair. A piece of cloth was cut from the girl's petticoat.

The boy's hair was rolled up in the piece of cloth and it was then tied around with red silk. For twelve hours it was left this way, then the silk was untied and burned. The puridai took the rolled-up cloth and climbed slowly up to the top of a hill. There she gradually unwound the cloth and, as she held it up she slowly turned around, in turn facing in all directions. As she turned, she allowed the wind to take the hair and blow it away. When all the hair had gone, she shook the cloth and then knelt and buried it.

For several days the Gypsy girl was inconsolable after learning that her gaujo boy had suddenly gone away, without even saying goodbye. His family told her that he had received a wonderful job offer in a far-distant town and had been so excited he had left right away. The Gypsy tribe moved on, the girl going with them. Two years later she married a second cousin and happily raised a fine Gypsy family.

A friend of mine—a poshrat (half-blood Rom) like myself—told me of a time when he lived for a year or two with a Gypsy family. They traveled the roads and camped where they could. This was in the years following World War II, when the travelers' traditional way of life was coming to an end. Campgrounds, or *atchin' tans*, were not easy to find. Many farmers wouldn't let them camp; many villages wouldn't allow them to stop. But, he told me, they didn't suffer as much as he thought they would. It seemed to him that the Gypsies were able to make any atchin' tan comfortable. They might just pull off along the side of a road and camp under overhanging trees, or they might be made to stay overnight on the edge of the town dump, or on marshy land that no one cared for. Wherever it was, he said, the surroundings seemed to take on a special ambience that made him feel that they had picked the best campsite ever.

It took a long time for him to find out the reason for this. He had commented on it to an old Rom named Cliff, and Cliff had said, "Oh, yes. That's 'cos Matty takes care of us."

Matty was the tribe's shuvani. She was an old woman—my friend guessed she had to be nearly ninety years old—but she was still in wonderful health. Small and slight, she still stood straight and when she spoke, everyone listened. She smoked an old pipe, as many Gypsy women do, and when asked a question would always puff on it thoughtfully for several minutes before answering. When the wagons pulled off to camp for the night, old Matty would take a branch of besom and walk all around the camp sweeping outward, away from the vardos. Cliff told my friend that she was "Sweepin' away the *waffedi*." Brushing away the uncleanness, the badness. Whatever it was, said my friend, old Matty had the power to turn any place into a warm and cozy campground.

A Gypsy once told me that you make your own luck. In other words, you don't just hope to get "lucky"; you work at it so that you *are* "lucky." There are many examples of this making of luck to be found in Gypsy life. For example, when a Rom gets a new jacket or a shirt he will always put it on and button it up completely, even if he's not planning on wearing it right away.

He will never button it in order to put it away without having first put it on himself. In this way the luck is attached to him. In the same way, if a woman gets a new scarf, or diklo, she will immediately put it around her neck and tie it. Then she may remove it and fold it to put away, doing the same with any other article of clothing.

It is unproductive, so far as luck goes, to sweep dirt out of your door after the sun has gone down. Gypsies are great believers in spirits of all kinds, and know that these spirits are about after dark. It is therefore unwise, not to mention rude, to sweep dirt out when it could go into the face of a passing spirit!

Many Gypsies will never start a journey on a Friday, and will never conclude a bargain on a Friday, the day sacred to Parashakti (in India, the mother of the gods). Also, they will never use needles or scissors on that day. Leland explains that "the shears as emblematic of death are naturally antipathetic to Venus (for whom Friday is also sacred), the source of life." Leland also mentions that Roumanian Gypsies will never wash anything on a Saturday (*Gypsy Sorcery*, 1891).

Most English Gypsies subscribe to the belief that to give someone a pair of scissors will lead to "cutting" the friendship. It is necessary, therefore, to pay for the scissors, usually with a sixpence. If someone accidentally drops a pair of scissors and they stick into the floor, it is an indication that they will be leaving the house within the hour. Also, any wish that they have spoken prior to dropping the scissors will be fulfilled.

Luck can certainly be encouraged in many ways. Irish tinkers (not the same as Gypsies, and generally greatly disliked and mistrusted by true Rom) try to "force" luck by repeatedly stating what they want. If they want to buy a good horse at a horse fair, on the way there they will say: "I will buy a fine black mare. I will buy a fine black mare. I will buy a fine black mare." If they want to sell the baskets they've made, they will say: "I will sell all of my baskets. I will sell all of my baskets. I will sell all of my baskets." It is always a positive statement. Never "I hope to..." or "I wish..." but "I *will*...." Usually they make the statement three times, though some do the repetition three times three—nine times. I have not found any English Gypsies who do this.

Magic in Knots

Rope (*shello*) is very important to Gypsies, as it is to sailors, since it is used so much in their lives. The Gypsies of the Steppes of Asia were highly skilled in the making of grass rope, an art that is almost lost to the Rom now. It used to be a once-a-year tribal event. While the Rooted people (non-Gypsies) were harvesting hay, the Gypsies were harvesting meadowgrass for ropemaking. The grass was collected by the men, and the women twisted and rolled it into rope in 100-foot lengths. These lengths were then twisted into 3-ply rope, which made about a ¾-inch rope (with all the men and women working together). Then, if needed, two or three of these 3-plies were twisted together, producing a tremendously strong and durable rope. The whole operation took about three days, from start to finish. Extra rope was made for trade and sale.

The premier rope, made, kept, and cherished by the Rom, was horsehair rope. This was considered very magical and potent. All the best ponies had halters and lead lines made of horsehair rope. The rope was made from the tail hair and was braided, twisted, and woven by numerous techniques into beautiful works of art. Different colored hair could make patterns. Sometimes the hair was dyed, although this was considered "cheating." It was always best to get red from a red horse, and so on. Sometimes the horsehair was woven into bracelets, love tokens, hat bands, and so on.

The Gypsies' intimate connection with rope also made knots of special interest to them, leading to much lore and legend regarding magical knots, some of which I discussed in Chapter 5.

Sheepshank

This is a common knot, not exclusive to the Gypsies, but to the Rom it's known as the "Marriage Knot." This is, perhaps, because of the two loops working in unison—a yin/yang appearance—and because the two can become stronger together. It's often used in love magic and also left as a message to an intended lover.

The main object of the sheepshank is to shorten the rope without cutting it. It can be used to tighten loads on a wagon, and also to bridge a weakened section of rope. One of the advantages of it is that it can be tied in the middle of a rope, without access to the ends. The secret to tying it is to keep the rope in tension all the time.

Four Winds Knot

This knot forms the Romany version of a swastika, so revered in India, and sacred to the sun, fire, and the four directions. This knot is used in necklaces, on halters, and is an excellent tie for a diklo (scarf) worn with an open-necked shirt or blouse. It can also be used to tie a sash, as on a robe.

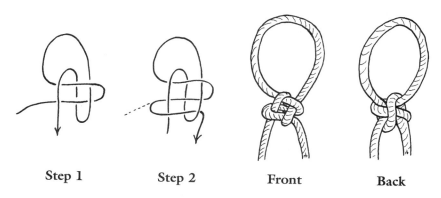

Step 1   Step 2   Front   Back

True Lovers Knot
This knot is often used to hang a talisman around the neck.

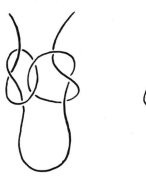

While tying any of these knots, it's customary to say the words: *Duvvel varter opré mandi* ("God watch over me").

9

PROTECTION AND EXORCISM:

Guarding Against Evil

Despite being looked upon by gaujos as "dirty" people, Gypsies are very clean and very much aware of the necessity for cleanliness. As I mentioned earlier, the scarcity of water is the reason they are sometimes unwashed. When it is difficult to get water, what is available is used for drinking and cooking, first and foremost. Certainly whenever the tribe comes to a river or stream, one of the first things they do is bathe in it. Gypsies also strive to be spiritually clean. They believe in such things as the evil eye, curses, black magic, and the like, and have many ways to cleanse and exorcise.

Gypsies do not curse people for the fun of it, as late-night movies and bad novels might have you believe! However, they will certainly not hesitate to turn a gaujo's negativity back on him or her. In this they differ from the Wiccans in that they will not sit back and wait for the gods to direct retribution—they will take matters into their own hands and act immediately. If they feel that evil has been directed at them, and they don't know from whom, they have ways of cleansing themselves of it. The Gypsy witch, the shuvani, is especially adept at this.

The Rom believe in the "evil eye." They believe that it is possible for someone to (in effect) put a curse on someone else merely by looking at that person. This may or may not be done deliberately, for there are those who possess the evil eye without even realizing it.

Roumanian Gypsies have a tradition of paying off the devil at a wedding, so that he will not put the evil eye on the marriage. This is accomplished by the bride placing a silver coin under her left arm and holding it there, with her arm tight against her body, for the duration of the ceremony. Then, as she and her new husband leave the wedding site, she will allow the coin to fall inconspicuously to the ground. Anyone who later finds the coin will enjoy seven years of good fortune, they say.

Many Gypsy children wear amulets (see Chapter 11) as a protection against the evil eye. The cowrie shell is a popular protective image. The cowrie is seen, universally, as a symbol of the female genitalia.

Leland suggests that anything associated with reproduction, generation, love, and pleasure is used to ward off evil since the latter "is allied to barrenness, destruction, negation, and every kind of pain and sterility" (*Gypsy Sorcery*, 1891).

A remedy for the evil eye, found among many Continental Gypsies, is to take a kettle to a stream and fill it with water, taken with the current, not against it. Seven pieces of coal are placed in the vessel, along with seven handsful of meal, and seven cloves of garlic. The kettle is put over a fire and the water brought to a boil. Then it is stirred with a three-forked stick and the following is said:

A Gypsy woman hawking her wares: amulets, talismans, clothespins, etc.

> Evil eyes that look on thee,
> May they here extinguished be!
> And then seven ravens
> Pluck out the evil eyes.
> Evil eyes now look on thee,
> May they soon extinguished be!
> Much dust in the eyes,
> So may they become blind.
> Evil eyes now look on thee,
> May they soon extinguished be!
> May they burn; may they burn,
> In the fire of all good!

To find out whether or not a baby has been "overlooked," that is, had the evil eye placed on it, a mother will take it to a stream and hold it out over the water, its face as close as possible to the stream. She then says:

Water, water, hasten!
Look up; look down.
Let as much water come into the eye
That looked evil on thee.
May it now perish.

If the sound of the running stream seems to get louder, then it's a sign that the child is, indeed, overlooked. If the stream just keeps running as before, then all is well and the child is safe.

There is another charm to get rid of the evil eye that I once saw performed by a shuvani in Cornwall. The "overlooked" person—in this case a rakli of about fourteen—was told to remove her clothes and lie flat on the ground with her head to the east. The old woman who was the shuvani had been to a nearby stream and filled a bottle with water. Into this she now put some salt. She stood for a long moment at the girl's head and seemed to be deep in thought. Then the shuvani started walking clockwise around the girl. As she walked she said the charm, and at the end of each line she filled her mouth with the salted water from the bottle and, leaning over, allowed it to trickle out of her mouth onto the rakli's body and limbs. She said:

Evil eyes see thee.
Like this water may they perish!
Sickness depart!
Go…from thy head,
From thy breast,
From thy belly,
From thy feet,
From thy hands.
May they go hence
Into the evil eye!

Salt is a universal symbol of new life and of purity, hence its use in baptismal water and the like. According to Ernest Jones ("The Symbolical Significance of Salt," in *Salt and the Alchemical Soul,* East Lansing, MI: Spring Publications, 1995) it symbolizes semen. Gypsies certainly use it as a purifier. If a coin (or any small item) is received from a gaujo who is thought to be evil or in any way "doubtful," it is placed in a bowl of salt for twenty-four hours to cleanse it of any negativity. This can, of course, be done with any object about which you have doubts concerning its psychic cleanliness.

If a person complains that their food is too salty when to everyone else it tastes fine, then it is suspected that there is some evil, or something evil, in that person and they are regarded with suspicion.

The use of a horseshoe to bring good luck and keep away evil is based on an old Gypsy folk tale. There were four demons named Unhappiness, Bad Luck, Ill Health, and Death. One evening a Gypsy was riding his favorite horse, traveling home in the gathering dusk when, as he crossed a bridge, the four demons came galloping out of the woods and started to chase him. The Gypsy managed to keep ahead of them as they raced across fields, jumped hedges, and ran along roads. But Bad Luck started to gain on him. The two horsemen drew away from the other three demons, and then, as they crossed a road, the Gypsy's horse threw a shoe. The horseshoe flew through the air and hit Bad Luck in the forehead, knocking him from his horse and killing him. The Gypsy stopped to pick up the shoe and continued on to his campground. The other three demons took their dead brother and buried him. The Gypsy nailed up the horseshoe over the door of his vardo, telling the rest of the tribe how it had killed Bad Luck. The next day the three demons came looking for the Gypsy but when they saw, hanging over the door, the horseshoe that had killed Bad Luck, they turned tail and fled.

If a Gypsy finds a horseshoe lying on the ground with its open end toward him and the calks pointing upward (the calks are the "toes" on the end of the shanks of the shoe), then he will pick it up and throw it over his left shoulder and spit, then continue on his way. If the open end is toward him with the calks down, he will pick up the shoe and hang it over the nearest tree branch or fence so that the bad luck may run out of it. He will again spit before continuing on. If the horseshoe is lying with the closed end toward him (calks up or down), it is a sign of good luck and he may, if he wishes, pick it up and take it home to hang over his door. Whether he takes the horseshoe with him or not, he will be lucky that day. A horseshoe should always, of course, be hung with the open end up and the closed end down to hold in the good luck.

Charles Bowness, in his book *Romany Magic* (York Beach, ME: Weiser, 1973), says that he knew a woman who would repeat the following words to get rid of disease in children:

Fire, fire, burn, burn!
From this child drive away
Disease and devils.
Drive away your smoke.

Give good luck to this child;
Make him lucky in the world.
Sticks and twigs and then more sticks
I give to you.
Fire, fire, burn, burn!

As Bowness points out, this is performed beside a small fire, where the shuvani repeatedly feeds the fire with sticks. I have seen something like this done to rid an old woman of a curse. The shuvani, in this case, had the old woman walk around the fire (since she was quite frail, she was assisted by her granddaughter) counterclockwise, while the spell was said. In this instance the words were slightly different:

Fire burn! Fire burn!
Let smoke and flame
Drive away all evil.
I add the wood, I add the sticks,
To bring the flame
That will drive away the devils.
Fire burn! Fire burn!

She said this three times in all. As she spoke the words, the shuvani threw something onto the fire that caused a flare-up of blue flame. I believe this substance was salt.

10

THE SIGHT:
Divination

Most gaujos picture the "typical" Gypsy gazing into a crystal ball! Certainly a number of Rom can and do *skry,* or crystal-gaze, but they have many other ways of divining the future. I dealt with some of them in my book *Secrets of Gypsy Fortunetelling* (St. Paul: Llewellyn, 1988).

Far more female Gypsies *dukker* (tell fortunes) than do males, but it is certainly not unknown, or even unusual, for a male Rom to do it, these days especially.

Leland felt that most if not all of the material produced by the *dukkerer* was the result of astute observation and invention, with a few lucky guesses. In *Gypsy Sorcery and Fortune Telling* (1891), he says:

> The gypsy fortune-teller is accustomed for years to look keenly and earnestly into the eyes of those whom she *dukkers* or "fortune-tells." She is accustomed to make ignorant and credulous or imaginative girls feel that her mysterious insight penetrates "with a power and with a sign" to their very souls. As she looks into their palms, and still more keenly into their eyes, while conversing volubly with perfect self-possession, ere long she observes that she has made a hit—has chanced upon some true passage or relation to the girl's life. This emboldens her. Unconsciously the Dream Spirit, or the Alter-Ego, is awakened. It calls forth from the hidden stores of Memory strange facts and associations, and with it arises the latent and often unconscious quickness of Perception, and the gypsy actually apprehends and utters things which are "wonderful." There is no clairvoyance, illumination or witchcraft in such cases.

Leland believed that probably ninety percent or more of what was presented by a Gypsy dukkerer was obtained by careful observation, experience, and artifice.

That experience and observation play a part is without question, to my mind, but that they play the major role I would seriously question. As anyone can tell who has read tarot cards, done astrological charts, read palms, or indulged in any of the dozens of popular forms of divination, there is far more to it than can be so easily explained. Facts are revealed, places are identified, people are named, accurately and without hesitation.

Where this information comes from, *no one*—to date—has been able to say and prove. Divining, by definition, is reading the past, present, and future from signs and portents, sometimes using objects (such as cards, crystal balls, or rune stones) for focal points, and sometimes not.

It is true that divination *can* be faked, as *can* most things. People who do not have the "gift" (more accurately, who do not have the patience to develop their natural abilities) can give a very credible performance along the lines of Leland's thinking, but that is *not* the same as actually divining. This is where such people as James Randi, Milbourne Christopher, and others fall on their faces, assuming that because something can be duplicated artificially, *all* such cases must be fraudulent. Elwood B. Trigg, in *Gypsy Demons and Divinities* (1973) says:

> Gypsies do indeed have shovanis who have stood out for their remarkable prophetic abilities.... (One such was) Urania Boswell. Born in 1852, and dying in 1933, she spent much of her life exercising her remarkable fortune-telling powers for gorgios. Her powers of divination, however, impressed not only gorgios but also her own people. She seemed to have a special sensitivity to impending danger or death. Not only predicting accurately the time of her son's and her brother's deaths, she also foresaw her own death nine years before it took place. The high points of her prophetic career were reached when she predicted accurately not only the year of Queen Victoria's death, four years before it actually happened, but also the development of airplanes, submarines and radio.

The Rom don't have to impress the critics. They draw repeat clients by providing information that is accurate. If a Romany woman goes into a village to tell fortunes and does not produce good, authentic material from the first reading, the rest of the village will know it in no time and she'll do no more business. For generations the Romany women have not only been accepted as good dukkerers, but have been eagerly looked for and sought after.

Many critics have made the point that Gypsy dukkerers will read for gaujos but are seldom, if ever, found reading for other Romanies. From this the conclusion is reached that there can be no truth in what is "seen" by the dukkerer. Surely, it is suggested, the Rom do not read for one another because they know it's all fake! But this is not so. First of all, on occasion the Rom *do* read for one another. It is, however, rarely that they do so. The reason is simply that the Gypsy, generally, has no interest in the future. The Gypsy philosophy is to live for the day. In fact, many tribes do not even have a Romanes word for "tomorrow" (this is not true of all, though—many do use *kolliko,* or *kolliko divvus,* meaning "tomorrow"). One of the reasons that the dukkerer seldom reads for his or her brother or sister is simply that there is no great interest or demand.

Slavic Gypsies divine with the aid of beans. The Client is asked for a coin and this is held in the Reader's hands, along with a number of dried beans. The beans and coin are shaken up while the Reader concentrates on any question being asked, and then the hands are opened and the beans and coin are allowed to fall on the table or ground. The coin represents the Client and the positions of the beans in relation to this are then interpreted. There are nine beans. When they fall on the ground, the area immediately in front of the Reader represents the present; the area farther away, the future. Two, three, or more beans lying close together indicate very powerful forces. Beans in a straight line mean a journey; those in a curved line, a problem or delay. Three beans in a triangular shape indicate a woman, and four beans in a square indicate a man.

Similar to this is the divination with stones I give in *Secrets of Gypsy Fortunetelling* (1988). For that you mark a circle in the dirt (or draw it on a large piece of paper), about eighteen inches in diameter, with a line down the center bisecting it. Across, at right angles to the main line, draw two lines dividing the circle into three. Looking at these horizontal lines, the closest segment to you represents the present; the center section is the near future; the farthest section is the far future. This gives you an idea of time: when things you see will actually come to pass. I would say that the first segment, the present, actually covers from "today" on for six months, or even a year. The center section, the near future, would be within the next two to five years. And the farthest segment is the far future: beyond five years.

The main line, going vertically from you, represents you, the Reader (when you are reading for yourself). The closer to this line that any stone falls, the more directly it affects you. A stone falling out near the edge of the circle, well away from that central line, will have only a slight effect on you.

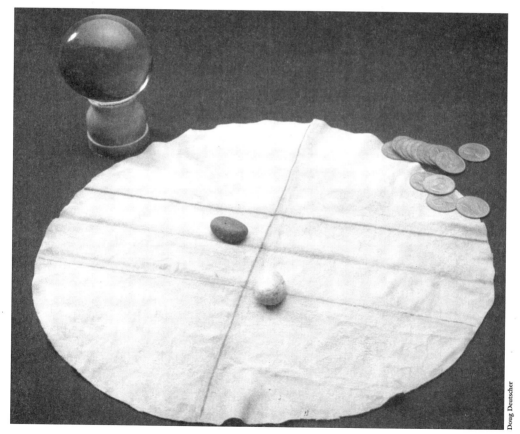

Throwing the stones, or *bars*, for divination.

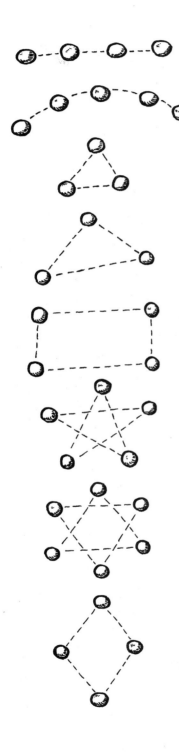

Three or more stones in a straight line—
    a JOURNEY

Three or more stones in a curved line—
    a SETBACK, or DELAY

A "tight" triangle—MONEY

A "loose" triangle—a WOMAN

A rectangle—a MAN

A five-stone star—GOOD LUCK

A six-stone star—BUSINESS SUCCESS

A diamond—TROUBLE WITH THE LAW

For this form of divination, as well as the method using the colored precious and semi-precious stones detailed in *Secrets of Gypsy Fortunetelling* (1988), you can also work with nine pebbles in the same way that the Slavic Gypsies work with their beans. These are small pebbles that you have collected just for this purpose. If you are doing a reading for someone else, then ask for and use a coin, as in the Slavic bean method above, and ignore the main vertical line. If you are reading for yourself, don't bother with a coin, just let that main vertical line represent you. When you throw the stones you are looking for patterns shown on the opposite page.

TAROT READING

Gypsies are also well known as readers of cards. The tarot deck almost certainly accompanied them out of India and was introduced into Europe in the eleventh and twelfth centuries. Today's modern playing cards, of course, come from the Minor Arcana of the tarot deck, with the suit of cups becoming hearts, pentacles becoming diamonds, swords becoming spades and wands becoming clubs.

Today there are several hundred different tarot decks on the market; I have heard one estimate of over two thousand! Many are variations on the basic Rider-Waite deck, others seem to be different just for the sake of being different! Artwork varies from incredibly beautiful and intricate to base and childlike. As to which deck you use— the choice is yours. I would suggest trying a number of different decks to find the one you most enjoy. The deck is made up of two parts, the Major Arcana and the Minor Arcana.

The twenty-two cards of the Major Arcana show various allegorical figures, such as Death, The Hierophant, The High Priestess, The Hermit, etc. The fifty-six cards of the Minor Arcana are divided into four suits: cups (sometimes called goblets or chalices), pentacles (coins, wheels, or circles), wands (scepters or staves), and swords. Each runs Ace through Ten, plus Page, Knight, Queen and King. In the Minor Arcana some decks simply show, for example, two swords, three swords, four swords, and so on through the suit, but other decks have whole scenes incorporating the two, three, or four swords, or whatever the card is. These "full scene" decks are by far the better choice for the beginner, giving you more symbols from which to interpret.

Today Gypsies can easily buy a deck of tarot cards, or use a regular card deck, but a few years ago there wasn't the proliferation of tarot decks that there is today. Many times you would see a Gypsy reading with a mixture of old tarot cards and playing cards. Sometimes missing cards from a tarot deck would be filled out with handmade cards. Occasionally the entire deck would be homemade.

When I was a small child I remember my Romany grandmother—who was seldom seen without a deck of cards in her hands—using a deck where all the Major Arcana cards were homemade. But they were not the traditional tarot figures; they were scenes from Gypsy life. Of the Minor Arcana, the Kings, Queens and Jacks were all Gypsy figures and the Aces bore pictures of various vardos. I have never forgotten those cards and, in the late 1980s, I finally reproduced them for my *Buckland Gypsy Fortunetelling Deck* (St. Paul: Llewellyn, 1989).

There are many books available on reading tarot cards and playing cards (see the bibliography), including a section in my *Secrets of Gypsy Fortunetelling* (1988). In that book I show a number of different spreads that are used by Gypsies. The following are two or three more that I have encountered, used by the Rom in various parts of Great Britain and France.

Thirty Plus

After shuffling and cutting the cards, the Reader takes the top and bottom cards from the deck and puts them to one side. This is sometimes referred to as "the surprise." Now three cards are dealt, face down, in a line across, right to left. Three more are placed on top of those, then three more, and so on—each time laid down from right to left—until there are ten cards in each of the three piles. The left-hand pile is representative of the Past, the middle is the Present, and the right is the Future.

The ten cards of the Past are taken up and laid out left to right, face up in a row, and interpreted. Following that, the Present ten are laid out beneath them and read. Then the Future cards are laid out

Dukkerin' a Gaujo Lady.

and read. Finally, the two cards constituting "the surprise" are turned over. They represent a sudden turn of events which will have a direct bearing on the future. In other words, the ten Future cards represent the future as it is most likely to be, with the forces at work at the time of the reading. But the two "surprise cards" show an unexpected force that may very well come into play and should therefore be prepared for.

Gypsy Threes

When using a regular deck, rather than a tarot deck, many times a Gypsy will only use thirty-two of the cards. This is referred to as the Continental method (as opposed to the English method, with fifty-two cards). The cards two, three, four, five, and six of each suit are removed, leaving the Aces, sevens, eights, nines, tens, Jacks, Queens, and Kings—thirty-two cards in all. (One advantage of this, of course, is that you have fewer meanings to remember.) The same thing can be done with the Minor Arcana of the tarot, although the Knight would also have to be removed. The resulting thirty-two-card deck should be shuffled and then cut, with the left hand, into three piles. As you pick them up, the center pile is placed under the right-hand pile and the left-hand pile goes on top of them all.

Turning the pack so that you can see the face of the bottom card, spread the bottom three cards and pull out the one of highest value, putting the other two to one side. Continue in this fashion, removing the highest valued card of each three and placing the other two on one side.

All the sets of two laid-aside cards should be shuffled together. Look through them and if there are any sets of three of any value or suit (three sevens, three tens, three diamonds, three hearts, etc.) all together, then pull them out and place them to the right of the original chosen cards. Now spread those original chosen cards, with the sets of three to their right. Read the cards from left to right.

Six Piles

This is also done using the thirty-two-card deck. Use a King, Queen, or Jack/Page to represent the Client. Usually a black-haired or very dark-haired person is represented by a spade (sword); a medium-brown-haired person by a club (wand); a light-brown-haired person by a diamond (pentacle); and a very fair-haired person by a heart (cup). Kings are for men, of course, and Queens for women. If the person is very young, then use the Jacks/Pages for both men and women. Place this "Significator" in the center of the table.

After the Client has fully shuffled the deck, deal out the first six cards in a circle around the Significator. Go around again and then a third time, so that you have six piles of three cards each. The piles are numbered clockwise from where you started (most start dealing at the top right), so that No. 1 position deals with Yourself (or the Client) and your personal events; No. 2 position is Your House (family; home affairs), No. 3 is your Friend (especially close friend); No. 4 is Your Work; No. 5 is What Lies Nearest Your Heart; and No. 6 is What Is Coming Soon (the immediate future). Turn over each group of three cards and interpret with regard to the meaning of its position.

'Gyptian Pyramid

This is done with either a full deck of fifty-two cards, or the full tarot deck. Shuffle the deck and cut it once with the left hand (in cartomancy—card reading—cuts are always made with the left hand, to the left). Taking the larger of the two piles, lay down the top card, face up. Underneath this place the next two cards, three below them, and four below those. Continue in this way, gradually increasing by one card in each line, until you have used all the cards from that pile. If you have been left with an incomplete row, then finish that row (only) with cards from the other, smaller, pile.

Now, from each row, pick up the last card in that row. This means that, at the top, you take away the single card there. The row below it, which was two cards, will now be a single card. Of those cards you have picked up, sort them into suits (disregard Major Arcana cards, if you are using a tarot deck) and see which suit has the most cards. If it is hearts/cups, then good luck will abound. If it is spades/swords, then bad luck will be in evidence. With diamonds/ pentacles, there will be good financial luck. Clubs/wands indicates the possibility of an affair. If there are two suits, each with the same number of cards in them (and more than the others), then draw one card at a time from the discarded cards (left over, in the smaller pile, after finishing off the pyramid) until you turn up one of the two suits.

Now take the end cards down the left side of the pyramid, put them together with the cards of the "winning"suit, and interpret all of them as a fortune for the Client.

Trin Putchipens (Three Questions)

This again uses the deck of only thirty-two cards. It seems a little complicated but is good for answering three questions. The Client should wish three wishes while shuffling the deck. The Reader then takes the top three cards off the deck and lays them in a row, face down. For the second row, below the first, five cards are dealt. Below them, seven cards are dealt.

Turn over the top row and add the numerical values (Ace is one, eleven for Jack/Page, twelve for Queen and thirteen for King). If one of the three cards is an Ace, then the first wish will certainly be granted. The highest value could be thirty-nine. From three to thirty-nine, judge the likelihood of the wish being granted—the lower the number, the better the chances.

Turn over the second row of five cards and judge the same way. Similarly with the third row of seven cards, though here two Aces would be needed to guarantee absolute success. In any row, a number of sevens and eights (the lowest value cards after Aces) are very good signs of success.

Lucky Aces

This is done for a quick sign of good luck for up to four people at one time. The Reader allots one Ace to each of the four. They know which suit is theirs and return the cards to the deck. Now each of the four clients takes a turn shuffling the deck while concentrating on their wish.

The first of the four clients now deals out, face up, thirteen cards. If there is an Ace among them, whoever had that Ace will *certainly* have his or her wish granted. If more than one Ace turns up, then the same thing applies to those. The Ace(s) is removed and the remaining cards returned to the deck, which is now again shuffled by all four people. The second person now turns up thirteen cards and again, if there is an Ace(s), that person's wish will *probably* be granted. That Ace, if there is one, is removed and again the cards are returned to the deck and everyone shuffles. If there are still Aces in the deck, then the third person will deal out thirteen cards and any Ace will again signify the possibility of good luck. A fourth deal is not permitted. Any Aces remaining indicate that there will be hard times in trying to make those particular wishes come true.

If a Gypsy doesn't happen to have any cards available but wants to dukker, then she or he will do so with coins. It seems probable that this system owes much to the ancient Chinese I-Ching which, although traditionally done with yarrow stalks, can also be done using three coins. Three is a magical, mystical number and it is three coins that are used by the Rom.

Doug Deutscher

Tools of Gypsy divination: cards, dice, dominoes, coins, and knife spinning.

It used to be that the dukkerer would ask the sitter for three silver or even gold coins. Today, any three coins are used. The coins should, however, all be of the same size and denomination.

The sitter holds the coins between her hands and concentrates on any question(s). Then they are passed to the reader who also holds them for a few moments, absorbing the energies. Then the coins are thrown down and their relative positions are noted. The separation of the coins, their distances from one another, and the patterns they assume are all relevant, but, for the purposes of this book, I will just give the basic "heads/tails" interpretation. For this, wherever the coins have fallen they are regarded as being in or close to a straight line. There are, then, eight possible combinations that may be observed:

HEAD	TAIL	TAIL
HEAD	HEAD	TAIL
HEAD	HEAD	HEAD
TAIL	TAIL	TAIL
TAIL	TAIL	HEAD
TAIL	HEAD	HEAD
HEAD	TAIL	HEAD
TAIL	HEAD	TAIL

These, again, may be equated with the eight trigrams of the I-Ching, but the way the Rom interpret them is as follows.

- Head–Tail–Tail—Possibly negative. Possibility of trickery. Be on your guard. Plan carefully. Bad investments. Opportunities, if you choose carefully.

- Head–Head–Tail—Possibly positive. Potential for gain. Chance to invest. Possibility of love.

- Head–Head–Head—Definitely positive. Joy and contentment. Wishes fulfilled. Enjoy yourself. Fertility.

- Tail–Tail–Tail—Definitely negative. Tragedy. Bad luck. Fraud. Scandal. Seduction.

- Tail–Tail–Head—Possibly negative. Exercise caution. Possibility of bad news. Financial loss. Accusations.

- Tail–Head–Head—Possibly positive. A letter containing good news. Meeting with an old friend. Business success. Inheritance.

- Head–Tail–Head—Possibly positive. Meeting with a man that could be very fortunate. A new beginning; chance to start over.

- Tail–Head–Tail—Possibly negative. Meeting with a woman. Plan before acting. Temptation.

There is, as I say, a much fuller, more complex divination possible with coins. The reading I've just described is a basic, quick-read method. Coin reading is not common among the Rom, but certain tribes do it and some dukkerers even do it exclusively.

MOLE READING

Some shuvanis will predict the future of a child by the moles on his or her body. Since they are birthmarks, their positioning is deemed significant. Not only is the position important, but the shape also has meaning.

Large moles are more significant than smaller ones. A round mole is fortunate; the more perfect the roundness, the greater the fortune. A pointed mole is unfortunate. It is exceptionally so if it has two or more points. If there is any particular shape to the mole, reminding the reader of an animal or object, this is interpreted. If the mole is large and raised, it is a sign of great potential. If the mole is hairy, it is an extremely negative sign. A light-colored mole is far luckier than a dark-colored one. Positions are as follows:

- Head, above the eyebrows: On the right—great intelligence; potential for fame and fortune. On the left—extravagance, irresponsibility. In the center—honors; wealth; love.

- Eyebrows: Right—happiness; perseverance; possibility of early marriage. Left—unhappy marriage unless much effort put into it.

- Eyelid: Thriftiness. On the outer corners of the eyelid—honesty; reliability; forthrightness.

- Cheek: A serious and studious person. Right cheek—happiness; good marriage. Left—struggles and problems throughout life.

- Nose: Sexuality; good fortune; travel. A sincere friend.

- Mouth: Sensuality; happiness.

- Chin: Good luck; good fortune; prosperity. A loving disposition. Accept responsibility.

- Jaw: Ill health.

- Ears: Left—recklessness. Right—bravery.

- Throat: Ambitious; rich marriage.

- Neck: A hard life; many opportunities but many setbacks. On the front of the neck—unexpected fortune late in life.

- Shoulders: A difficult life with much hard work. Right—discreet; a faithful marriage and business partner. Left—Unambitious.

- Arms: Right—success. Left—money problems.

- Hands: Right—natural ability. Left—ability to learn easily.

- Chest: Right—many changes of fortune throughout life, but ending in wealth and happiness. Left—distraction and attraction with barely enough wealth.

- Ribs: Right—cowardice and insensitivity. Left—a slow developer and slow healer.

- Abdomen: Laziness; greed; self indulgence; tend to excess in eating and drinking.

- Back: Upper—generous but inclined to arrogance. Lower—sensuous; a lover.

- Hips: Strong, healthy children.

- Buttocks: A good sense of humor; accepting of life, whether good or bad.

- Thighs: Right—happiness in marriage; wealth and health. Left—loss; loneliness; poverty, but optimistic.

- Knees: Right—handle finances easily. Left—rash and frivolous.

- Lower Legs: Right—refined; good sense of dress. Left—casual but elegant.

- Ankles: Hard worker; good provider. On a man, a fearful, timorous nature; on a woman, willingness to share all.

- Feet: Right—love of travel. Left—fear of travel.

RADIESTHESIA

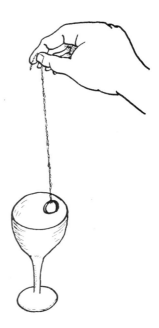

Radiesthesia technique.

Radiesthesia—divination with a pendulum—is often used by shuvanis. They will frequently use a ring from their finger or a pendant from around their neck. The pendant, of course, is allowed to hang from its chain. A ring is suspended on the end of a length of red or green silk thread. The favored technique is to hold the chain or thread between the first finger and thumb, and allow the weight to hang suspended in the top of a wine glass. Questions are asked and the weight will swing in response, striking against the side of the glass. One strike for "Yes" and two strikes for "No" is usual. It can also spell out initials or even whole words, by chinking against the glass 1 for A, 2 for B, 3 for C, and so on. This can be time consuming, so the Yes/No response is more usually sought. If reading for someone else, the reader will ask for and use a ring or pendant belonging to the sitter.

There are many, many more forms of divination used by Gypsies. Some are governed by their surroundings, the resources available to them, or their inventiveness. Some of the forms mentioned may be found used by Gypsies of one area but not another; some seem to be used by all Gypsies. However, all Gypsies acknowledge having the ability to divine—an ability we all have but don't always recognize—and they do not hesitate to develop their powers.

II

MAGICAL AIDS:
Amulets and Talismans

mulets and talismans are of all sorts. Amulets are *natural* items, either naturally imbued with magical powers or artificially charged with power. Talismans are *manmade* objects charged with magical power. An example of an amulet would be a stone with a natural hole through it, or a rabbit's foot. An example of a talisman would be a piece of parchment, or a coin, on which have been written certain symbols or words of power. Gypsies use both, though even their talismans are often based on natural, found objects.

I have mentioned the putsi, or pouch, one of the most common things a Gypsy carries. Many Rom's putsis serve as ordinary pouches, often attached to their belts, that hold all sorts of odds and ends. But many times, too, a putsi holds magical charms—amulets and/or talismans. The putsi may be large or small, and it can be made of any material. Most are of cloth, although some are leather. You might see a Gypsy woman wearing what looks like a small cloth pouch hanging from a cord about her neck. To the gaujo it looks like an accessory to her colorful dress, but in fact it contains magical items that make it a powerful talisman for the woman.

CHARMS

Charms—as I will call both amulets and talismans—are made for all sorts of things, but usually they fall under one or more of the following headings: Protection, Health, Wealth, Love, or Power. Certain items are associated with each of these headings. I have found the following items used in magical pouches all across England and in many parts of the rest of Europe.

Protection

Salt	Iron	Thorns
Acorn	Cat's claw	Hedgehog bristles
Pewter	Urine	Teeth (bear, boar, fox, wolf)
Mirror	Horseshoe nail	Lemon peel
Small bones	Rabbit's paw	Tortoise shell

Herbs: African Violet, Agrimony, Ague Root, Aloe, Anemone, Angelica, Anise, Basil, Bittersweet, Boneset, Buckthorn, Caraway, Cinnamon, Cinquefoil, Cumin, Dill, Dragon's Blood, Fennel, Fleabane, Garlic, Heather, Hyssop, Irish Moss, Juniper, Lavender, Linden, Mandrake, Mugwort, Myrrh, Nettle, Orris Root, Parsley, Pennyroyal, Plantain, Ragwort, Rowan, Sage, St. John's Wort, Thistle, Valerian, Vervain, Wild Thyme, Witch Hazel, Wood Betony.

Stones: Amethyst, Black Tourmaline, Bloodstone, Carnelian, Cat's Eye, Chrysoberyl, Chrysolite, Coral, Emerald, Garnet, Jacinth, Jade, Jasper, Jet, Lapis Lingurius, Malachite, Moonstone, Onyx, Opal, Quartz Crystal, Sapphire, Sard, Sardonyx, Topaz, Turquoise.

Health

Acorn	Horseshoe nail	Red flannel
Sheep's wool	Snakeskin	Eel skin
Fox fur	Walnut	Horse chestnut/Buckeye
White stone	Gold coin	Small bones

Herbs: Allspice, Anemone, Angelica, Camphor, Coriander, Cornflower, Fennel, Groundseal, Juniper, Larkspur, Life-Everlasting, Marjoram, Mugwort, Mullein, Nutmeg, Parsley, Plantain, Rosemary, Rue, Sage, Sassafras, Solomon's Seal, Spikenard, St. John's Wort, Thyme, Walnut, Wood Sorrel.

Stones: Agate, Amber, Amethyst, Beryl, Bloodstone, Carbuncle, Carnelian, Chalcedony, Chrysolite, Coral, Diamond, Emerald, Garnet, Jade, Jasper, Lapis Lazuli, Lodestone, Malachite, Moonstone, Opal, Pearl, Peridot, Rose Quartz, Ruby, Sapphire, Sardonyx, Topaz, Turquoise, Zircon.

Wealth

Squirrel fur	Rabbit's foot	Silver coin
Magnet	Glass beads	Gold coin
Lodestone	Acorn	Magnifying glass
Die or dice		

Herbs: Alfalfa, Allspice, Almond, Basil, Bladderwrack, Blue Flag, Cedar Chips, Chamomile, Cinnamon, Cinquefoil, Clover, Comfrey, Dill, Dock, Elder, Fenugreek, Flax, Ginger, Goldenrod, Golden Seal, High John the Conqueror, Honeysuckle, Irish Moss, Jasmine, Mandrake, Marjoram, May Apple, Mint, Myrtle, Nutmeg, Patchouly, Periwinkle, Poppy, Sesame, Tonka, Vervain, Woodruff.

Stones: Black Opal, Carbuncle, Coral, Diamond, Emerald, Green Tourmaline, Moonstone, Quartz Crystal, Rose Quartz, Ruby, Turquoise.

A Reading Vardo at Appleby Fair.

Love

Red or pink silk	Orange peel	Keys
Acorn	Mirror	Tea leaves
Walnut shell	Peas in a pod	Miniature horseshoe
Owl's feather	Gold ring	Red or pink silk
Mandrake Root	Snake egg	thread with three
Bell	Bird's egg	knots tied in it

Herbs: Basil, Bedstraw, Betony, Black Cohosh, Bloodroot, Caraway, Cardamon, Catnip, Chamomile, Cinnamon, Cinquefoil, Coltsfoot, Columbine, Coriander, Damiana, Dill, Dragon's Blood, Gentian, Ginseng, Hawthorn Berries, Hibiscus, High John the Conqueror, Jasmine, Juniper, Laurel Leaves, Lavender, Lemon Balm, Linden, Liverwort, Lovage, Love Seed, Maidenhair, Mallow, Mandrake, Marjoram, Mistletoe, Moonwort, Myrtle, Pea, Peppermint, Periwinkle, Poppy, Primrose, Rose, Rosemary, Rue, Saffron, Sarsaparilla, Scullcap, Senna, Spearmint, Strawberry, Thyme, Tonka, Valerian, Vervain, Violet, Witch Grass, Wormwood, Yarrow.

Stones: Aquamarine, Black Opal, Bloodstone, Cat's Eye, Diamond, Garnet, Lapis Lazuli, Moonstone, Onyx, Opal, Pearl, Pink Quartz, Ruby, Sardonyx.

Power

Horseshoe nail	Acorn	Animal teeth/claws
Gold coin	Iron	Black stone
Oak chip	Flint stone	

Herbs: Bladderwrack, Borage, Carnation, Cinnamon, Club Moss, Devil's Shoestring, Ebony, Flax, Gentian, Ginger, High John the Conqueror, Honeysuckle, Mace, Mandrake Root, Mastic, Mugwort, Rosemary, Rowan, Sage, Thyme, Vervain.

Stones: Alexandrite, Amazonite, Beryl, Bloodstone, Carbuncle, Chrysolite, Coral, Diamond, Garnet, Jade, Moonstone, Opal, Rock Crystal, Quartz Crystal, Topaz, Zircon.

In England's New Forest I encountered an old shuvano who had a pouch that he claimed was good for everything. It was a small cloth bag that had been sewn up, closing in its contents. Those contents, he told me, were a feather from a cuckoo, a stone that was half black and half white, an acorn, a horse chestnut, a horseshoe nail, a lock of hair from a red-headed woman, a piece of amber, a piece of jet, and a small packet of salt. He had good reason for the inclusion of every one of these items. There were nine items in the bag; he said that there should always be an odd number—never an even number.

AMULETS

Parts of animals are often worn or carried as amulets for protection from, or as a remedy for, disease. A snake skin, rolled up and tucked into a putsi, is often carried as a protection against snake bite, or as a cure for rheumatism. Burdock seed, carried in a pouch, is another good preventive for rheumatism, incidentally. Irene Soper tells how the New Forest Gypsies frequently wear a ring made from plaited hair taken from the mane and tail of one of the wild New Forest ponies. They had to be either piebald or skewbald ponies, and the rings would bring the wearer good luck. Also, carrying a piece of bread in the pocket, or in a putsi, would protect you from ghosts and evil spirits.

A woman in childbirth must have sprigs of garlic placed under her to protect her from the evil eye, or *waffedi yok*. Charms of jet or carved from horn are worn for the same protection. A young child will have his bath water poured over him, making the water run along the blade of a scythe as it falls. Then the child is given a horseshoe nail, on a cord, to wear. This is a sure protection against the evil eye.

Hungarian Gypsies believe that a woman wearing a necklace of the teeth and claws of a bear will have strong, healthy children. In Austria and Italy, boars' teeth are similarly worn.

One form of talisman that is used on Gypsy horses is the horse brass. This is a traditional design, made out of brass, that is hung around the horse's neck, or attached to some part of the harness to bring protection from disease and bad luck and to protect against the evil eye. (I will talk more about these in Chapter 14.)

A horseshoe nail is frequently used as a talisman. Sometimes the smith will bend such a nail into a circle, so that the head meets the point. This can be hung on a piece of leather or cord.

TALISMANS

Gypsy talismans may be made out of iron, wood, painted on stones, engraved on coins, or drawn on parchment. In *Secrets of Gypsy Love Magick* (1990), I described some of the ones made for success in love. I have repeated a few of them here and added to them. Coins are used a lot. Most coins can be easily engraved, using nothing more than a sharp nail.

Here are some of the symbols used by Gypsies. One or more of them might be painted on stone, carved or burned into wood, written on parchment, or engraved on coins. The wood used for Protection and for Power is hard wood, such as oak, ash, elm, beech, walnut, or maple. Soft woods are used for Love charms and also for Wealth. Wood from a tree that has been struck by lightning is ideal for a power charm.

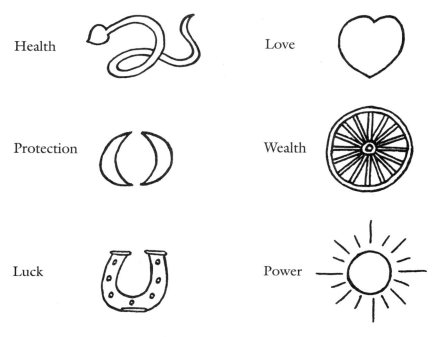

Health

Love

Protection

Wealth

Luck

Power

Examples of Talismanic Designs.

Among Gypsies, there is no general consensus on the consecration of talismans. Most Rom perform some action after making the object, but it seems to be on an individual basis. Many will simply hold the object in the waters of a running stream, perhaps saying a few spontaneous words, or repeating a generations-old verse. Others will bury the talisman in the ground for a period of time, then dig it

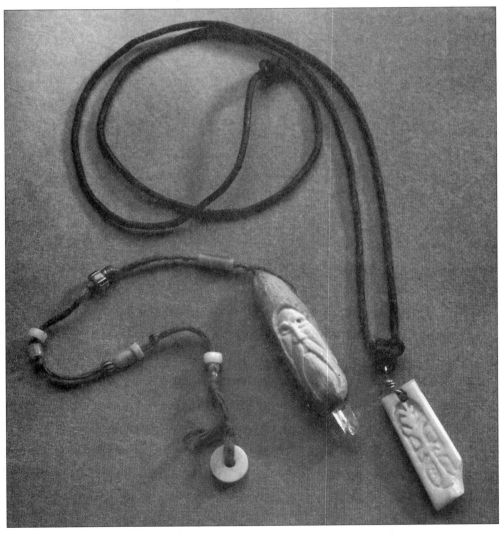

Doug Deutscher

Gypsy talismans. The talisman on the left is hand carved from bone. The one on the right, carved from an ivory piano key, is a tree or *Rook*, symbolizing strength and flexibility.

up and use it. Still others will hold it in the smoke of the campfire while saying words.

In previous chapters I have given some of the incantations used for such things as healings. Here are a few that I have found used for consecrating, or "blessing," a talisman.

Mi Duvvel opral, dik tele opré mande

My God above, look down upon me.

Si kovvel ajaw

The thing is so.

Guard me with this thing I show,
Keep away my strongest foe;
Place protection from all ills,
From my campfire to the hills.

*Gana sharraf, Gana varter, Gana
Akai 'sa mandi.*

Gana bless, Gana watch, Gana be
Here with me.

Gypsies, who are generally skilled at wood carving, will make special wooden beads for various occasions, to celebrate a birth or a wedding, for example. To carve your own bead, however simple, can be very powerful magic. A lot of energy goes into it, and by concentrating on the purpose of the bead—love, prosperity, health, for example—you direct that energy and generate the magical power. A whole necklace of beads made in this fashion can be very powerful, indeed. Some of the carved beads I've seen are incredibly intricate, calling for a tremendous amount of patience and skill. Plainer beads, of course, can be decorated by wood-burning or painting. Beads can be colored and significant colors used.

I once saw hanging in a vardo a beaded curtain made entirely of hollowed chicken bones, mostly from legs and wings. The bones were bleached white, then painted in bright colors.

Feathers are also used as amulets. A black feather means a change of plans, and can also signify a message from the gods. A white feather is for indecision—a need to make up your mind—or it can mean that you will soon have to make a choice of some sort. A red feather is a very lucky omen, a sign of great good fortune. A blue feather is one of protection, or is a hint that you might *need* protection. A brown feather is the feather of trust and friendship.

One final, and somewhat unusual, Gypsy magical aid is the *bok-moro*, or "luck bread." It is a cake baked with ingredients felt to have special significance. The recipe calls for flour, to represent the physical body; yeast, the rising spirit; water, the eternal; sugar, sweetness; egg, manifestation; garlic to take away evil; olive oil, the sacred; salt, to banish and cleanse; black pepper to purify; and honey for love and peace. Also placed in it is a coin, to pay for karma, and a pinch each of frankincense and myrrh. Proportions vary from tribe to tribe, and even from individual to individual, but basically it is all baked into a cake. It must, however, be baked at night, after sunset. The next morning, the cake is taken to the four corners of the atchin' tan, or camp site, and a small piece broken off and dropped on the ground. The rest of the cake is then broken up and scattered around the perimeter of the camp site, as an offering to the creatures who live all about the travelers.

12

SEXUAL MAGIC AND POWER:
Raw Energy from the Self

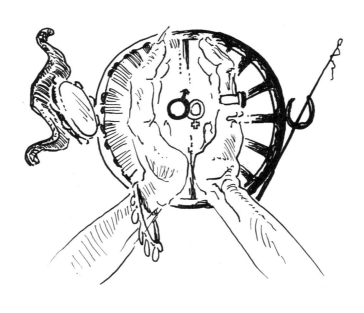

The majority of "civilized" people have been brainwashed from their earliest years to believe that sex is something shameful, "dirty," or "sinful." Sex is something that is never discussed—especially not in mixed company—and only referred to with mild euphemisms. Human beings only come in two models, male and female, but the one is not supposed to have knowledge of the other—especially the very young. Such is the state of "civilization."

The Rom are far advanced from much of the rest of the world in this respect. They accept sex for what it is—part of nature, part of our very being. It is not shameful; it is a joy! It is something to be celebrated. It should not be that the male and the female of the species are the antithesis of one another. Rather, they should, and do, complement one another. Neither is complete without the other.

The Gypsy family is close, physically, spiritually, and emotionally. Living together in a small vardo, a Gypsy family quickly comes to terms with all of its members. Oftimes mother, father, and all the children sleep together in one large bed. Certainly the children will sleep together. In growing up, therefore, the children come to know of the relationship between the sexes. Many chavvis have their first taste of the sexual experience with a sibling. It is not in any sense of "child abuse," but rather in the fullness of the expressions of love and true kinship.

This is actually not a unique lifestyle. In the Ozark regions of Missouri and Arkansas there are families of hillfolk who live in similar arrangements. Even some large farm families, across the United States and in many other parts of the world, live similar lifestyles. A closeness with nature, and particularly a close association with animals, breaks down the isolation that most others have experienced when it comes to being natural. These people live as a part of nature, rather than apart *from* nature.

So it is that Gypsies see the sense of utilizing sexual power as a magical aid. In *Buckland's Complete Book of Witchcraft* (Llewellyn,

1986), I talk about sex magic and its powerful forces, showing how these can be drawn upon. This is the way some Gypsy shuvanis work. In *Secrets of Sex Magic* (Llewellyn, 1995), Frater U∴D∴ says: "Every magician should be able to perform every form of sexuality, so that real freedom from attachments and ingrained patterns is guaranteed." Shuvanis would agree with that, since they do not hesitate to do whatever they consider necessary for the particular set of circumstances. B. Z. Goldberg's book *The Sacred Fire* (University Books, New York, 1958), is replete with examples of sexual magic being used—in early Christianity, primitive societies, and in classical times.

One way in which the Romany people work with sex magic is in the making of talismans and the use of amulets. It is not uncommon to "charge" these items with extra power through consecration with sexual secretions. Many women are able to ejaculate at the moment of orgasm and shuvanis seem to have mastered this technique. They can then consecrate items during magical rites involving ritual masturbation. Shuvanos, of course, consecrate with seminal fluid. Rom who consult a shuvani might be instructed to do this themselves, after making their own talisman. But it is seldom that a gaujo is so advised, since the Rom are well aware of the prejudice against sexual activity developed over many generations of Christian dominance.

Goldberg talks of the sex rites performed in their temples by the Kauchiluas people of India. He also speaks of the sexual aspects of the sacrifice of the Cartavaya to the Indian god Krishna and the Soma sacrifice in the Vedic ritual. Sex features prominently with the Hindus and in the worship of Siva and Sakti. The *lingam* and *yoni*, symbolizing the male and female sex organs, are everyday objects in India. It is no wonder, then, that the Gypsies, originating from that country, have such a refreshingly open mind on sexual matters. It is, perhaps, understandable that there are occasions when a shuvani or shuvano will have sexual relations with a "client" as part of the magical help being given.

One of the superstitions found among some Gypsies is that if the family runs out of salt, the sexual prowess of the Rom will be affected. Salt, of course, is associated with sex in many cultures around the world. Salt symbolizes semen; it symbolizes life itself. Even Christian baptismal water is no more than water with salt added. A woman wishing to conceive may be told to put a small bag of salt, together with other items, into a putsi she is to wear. An old charm to draw a virile young man to a woman is for her to walk backwards, naked, around her vardo or house, in the light of the full moon, sprinkling salt on the floor behind her.

One very powerful and effective spell is called *kitan-epen*, which means "togetherness." It is used to bring and keep a couple close, not only in love but also in friendship. Male and female Gypsies usually have a diklo, or scarf, that may be worn around the head or around the neck. For this spell, the couple will make love wearing nothing but their diklos. After the act, each will then use the scarf to wipe the genital areas, being sure to get sexual secretions onto the material. The diklos are then placed one on top of the other and rolled up. The ends of the rolled scarfs are knotted and the conjoined diklos are put away in some safe place. On the wedding anniversary, or some other significant annual date, they are taken out and placed under the mattress while the couple again make love. This is guaranteed to keep love and friendship alive.

Shuvanis were, and still are, occasionally approached by farmers and asked how to make the fields or the animals more fertile. Until recent times—and probably still today, in some areas—the Gypsy witch would give advice that was common knowledge and practice back in the Middle Ages. The farmer would be advised to have intercourse with his wife in the first furrow plowed in a field, or in the barn where the animals were kept. This should be done in the waxing cycle of the moon, as close to the full moon as possible.

A similar spell was used to promote business for a businessman. He would be instructed to have sex with his wife in his store or office, on a night of the waxing moon.

Most sex magic was connected to the phases of the moon—the waxing cycle for promoting and advancing, and the waning cycle for depleting and ridding. Masturbation and autoerotic practices were recommended where necessary. Homosexual practices were never frowned on by the Rom.

A woman in love may make a necklace of clay beads into which she has worked some of her menstrual blood. At night she will creep out and leave the string of beads at the foot of the steps up to her lover's vardo. If they have completely dissolved by daybreak, then he is not the right man for her. Some Gypsy men have been known to do the same thing, using semen in the beads and placing them at the foot of the woman's vardo.

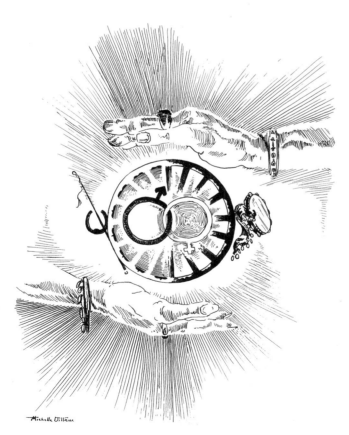

An artist's symbolic rendition of the Gypsy spell called *kitan-epen*.

13

CHAVVIS:

Romany Children

Francis Groome, writing in the late 1870s (*In Gypsy Tents*, London: Nimmo, 1880), said of Gypsy children that they were "odd compounds of pluck and shyness, of cheek and courtesy, of thoughtlessness and meditation, of quicksilver gaiety and quaint old-fashionedness."

In *The Gypsies, Waggon Time and After* (London: Batsford, 1975), Denis Harvey says:

> Gypsy children have ever been indulged and allowed plenty of freedom. Nevertheless they had their routine chores such as *kettering coshties* (collecting firewood), harness-cleaning and water-carrying. Lacking sophisticated toys, their play was closely bound up with nature and animals, and with emulating the work activities of parents and older brothers and sisters. This fostered the spontaneous growth of intelligence and awareness and was sound preparation for the independent livelihood of the roads.

Children are a part of every Gypsy family and there is a tremendous closeness of family—far more so than is found in gaujo society, it seems. A pregnant woman is treated with every consideration by the whole tribe. Among the French travelers, the tribal leader, or "Gypsy King," often keeps various ancient icons of sacred significance bearing pictures of deities and royalty of great beauty. These are loaned to the expectant mother (and to no one else), so that she will be surrounded by these and other items of beauty while carrying the baby. It is believed that this will bring about a beautiful child. This is, incidentally, a custom mentioned in the *Kama Sutra*.

Most Gypsy women work right up to the moment of delivery. Clébert says that some French Gypsy women will even go into the bender tent (built for this purpose) to deliver by themselves, often standing upright with legs apart (1967). In contrast, among Slavic

Gypsies the woman is confined to bed as early as six weeks before the birth. More commonly the woman continues as normal but with some attention given at the time of delivery, which is overseen by the woman's mother and by the puridai of the tribe. They will see to unknotting any ties in her clothing, loosening her hair, and symbolically removing all restrictions. They will also bring her food and drink while she remains in the tent.

Mokkadi is the Romanes word for "unclean," especially in the sense of taboo. A woman who is in childbirth is mokkadi, which is why she must be isolated in a bender tent and not allowed into the vardo at that time. She is provided with her own dishes and cutlery, which must be washed separately from everyone else's. She may not be seen by any men, including her husband, until some time after the child has been born—anywhere from three days to three weeks. Although other women may visit, they may not touch either the mother or the baby, for fear of themselves becoming mokkadi.

In Scotland and on the Continent, if the woman has trouble delivering, the puridai will drop an egg between the woman's legs while chanting:

> *Youra, tikni youra si kolo;*
> *Sor si kolo.*
> *Chavvi, av adré sasteem.*
> *Duvvel, mi-duvvel, tutti milos.*

> The egg, the little egg is round;
> All is round.
> Little child, come in health.
> God, God is calling you.

In Germany, according to Clébert, a woman having difficulty delivering is made to drink water in which three eggs have been boiled. The eggs themselves are eaten by her husband. If a woman should die in childbirth, she is buried with an egg under each arm. This is said to prevent vampires from feeding on her milk. The following is chanted:

> When this egg shall be decayed,
> Here will there be no milk!

Gypsy women and children inside a bender tent.

The hair of a redheaded woman is magical in many ways. To carry a lock of such hair in a putsi, worn next to the skin of her belly during pregnancy, will guarantee a woman an easy delivery and a healthy child. Red hair is known as *kam-bal*, or "sun hair."

There seems to be little disciplining of children in Gypsy families. They are allowed to learn by doing. From quite an early age they will go hawking, from door to door, with their parents. They have little in the way of toys but are wonderful at improvising. Gypsy chavvis seem to have no trouble entertaining themselves.

Some Gypsies believe that, for good luck, a newborn boy should be wrapped in an old shirt of the father's or, if a girl, a petticoat of the mother's. Welsh Gypsies will give children water from a stream to drink in a thimble. This is supposed to help with teething. One family of Welsh Gypies also said that you should never tickle a baby under the chin; it will cause the child to stammer later in life.

Women will make clay beads of different designs, which can be powerful talismans for childbirth. These beads may or may not be fired. Young girls, at their first menstration, will make clay beads into which they mix that first menstrual blood. These, for whatever reason, are called *sap* beads, or "snake" beads. This is a charm against pregnancy and the girl will then wear the beads, or keep them safe, until such time as she desires to be pregnant. Then she will take the sap beads and go alone to a stream. There she will toss the beads into the water and make a wish for pregnancy as the beads slowly dissolve in the water. (The beads are tossed into the water well downstream from where the family draws their water, for reasons of mokkadi.) Releasing magical power in this manner is not uncommon. Many shuvanis will work power into clay beads and later release the power by dissolving the beads in water.

At the birth of a baby, some of the umbilical cord and blood is worked into a clay bead. The bead is given to the child at his or her coming of age and is kept and treasured for life. At the person's death, the bead is dissolved, releasing their spirit. These are often called *zee* beads, or "soul" beads.

A Gypsy boy is considered to be an adult at fourteen years of age. At that time he will construct a birdhouse with wood and bark that he has collected in the forests.

A birdhouse.

The birdhouse is much like a Bow Top vardo in shape. The boy will carve his name, initials, or mark into it and will then go deep into the woods and hang the birdhouse high in a tree. Offerings are left in it. The next time the family passes that way, the boy will check the house. If a bird has nested in it, it is a sign that the *chirilo* (bird) is watching over the boy's spirit. Birds are revered as messengers of spirit, as symbols of sun, wind, sky and spirit, and as guardians of the trees.

Children—girls as well as boys—will often make birdhouses to sell in the towns and villages, but those birdhouses are not the same design as the one built by the boy at the time of becoming a man. The birdhouses to be sold are constructed of scrap wood and are made with much less care than those marking adulthood.

At fourteen, a boy will also make a knife (*chiv* or *choori*) for himself. This is often made from an old file or cut from an old saw blade. It is shaped like a small sickle and the tang is fitted into a slot in a hand-carved, wooden handle. This is used for making wooden flowers, clothespins, and for any other tasks around the campsite.

A *choori* (knife).

Gypsies the world over love their cup of tea. Many make the tea themselves, and one of the earliest chores for a chavvi is to collect the herbs for the tea. There are what might be termed "afternoon teas," such as lavender, lemon grass, lemon verbena, peppermint, Bahe-Bahe; "spring teas," such as pennyroyal, sassafras, and sarsaparilla; full-flavored teas such as bee balm, dictamnus, and sage. Raspberry leaf tea is an old standby, very popular in most of England. Red clover flower is similarly popular. Rose hip tea, parsley, black currant leaf, catnip, betony—the list goes on and on.

Chavvis will also be sent out to collect some of the spices that can be used to prevent food becoming rancid. It has long been assumed that many spices were used to *cover up* any rancid taste to food, but the Gypsies have found ways to use spices that actually preserve fats under various circumstances that would normally turn food rancid. These spices include caraway, cinnamon, cloves, cumin, fennel seed, nutmeg, pepper, and turmeric. Fennel is often used with fish.

Gypsies will add a handful of oats to give coffee an extra flavor. The oats are boiled up for fifteen minutes in a quart of water, then the water is strained off and thrown away. The oats are then immersed in another quart of water and boiled for thirty minutes. Again the liquid is strained off but this time the oats are discarded. The coffee is then made with this last liquid. The resulting coffee has a vanilla-like taste to it, which is very pleasant.

Many Gypsy women smoke a pipe. They frequently make their own tobacco mixtures. Coltsfoot, mixed with betony, rosemary, thyme, lavender, chamomile, and eyebright, is a favorite. Others, smoked by themselves or mixed, are: chervil, life everlasting, mullein, rosemary, and sage. Allspice can be mixed with regular tobacco, as can deer tongue, licorice, marjoram, master-of-the-woods, and styrax.

14

FUR AND FEATHERS:
Animal Love and Healing

Living so close to nature, it is only natural that there is a tremendous bond between the Gypsies and all forms of animal life. It is said that man's best friend is the dog. The Gypsy's best friend is his horse, or *grai*. He relies on the horse to pull his home and to help with work; he trades horses, and he keeps his horses in the best possible condition. Without a horse, it would be almost impossible for the Gypsy to move around. The most common decorative motif found carved into vardos is the horse. It is the Gypsy's emblem of the traveling life.

Gypsies used to have a good business trading in horses. Farmers used them, of course, but so did coaching and freight companies, the army, and the coal mines. It would seem that there is not the same demand now, but, in fact, there still is a good living to be made from horse trading. Today there are many riding schools, and horses are used for racing, breeding, hunting, and driving. The advantage that the Rom has is that he is his own veterinarian and blacksmith. He can save a lot of money by doing his own horse-doctoring and shoeing.

Every year, in the middle of June, a big horse fair is held in the north of England, at Appleby, beside the River Eden. There are other fairs— Brough Hill, Seamer, Lee Gap, Yarm, Malton, Topcliffe, and Barnaby, for example—but Appleby is always considered *the* horse fair. It has been held for well over 300 years. The horse trading at the fair was originally done on a stretch of ground known as the Sands, beside the river. Later, however, it was moved to Gallows Hill, where it still takes place today. As many as 5,000 people gather on the thirty-acre site each year.

With this closeness to horses it is no wonder that various superstitions have grown up around them, among the travelers. One such is that when horses' tails bush out, seeming very large and full, it is a sure sign that a drought is coming to an end. When a horse refuses to drink in very dry weather, it means that a cloudburst can soon be expected. Also, when horses start scratching themselves on trees and fences, it is a sign of approaching heavy rain.

There are different ways of telling what height a horse will become by looking at it when first foaled. One Gypsy in Northumberland told me that if you measure the height from the ground to the point of its shoulder, this will be just half of the height to which it will finally grow. It should be measured when the foal first stands on its four feet.

Many Gypsies believe that it is very bad luck to change a horse's name. If selling a horse, then, it is a dirty trick to tell the buyer that it's name is something other than what it has been. It is very *good* luck, apparently, to meet or even see a red-haired girl on a white horse.

Charles Leland says that Hungarian Gypsies have a spell they perform if a horse is stolen (1891). They will take some of the harness and bury it. Then, on that spot, they will light a fire and over it say:

> Who stole thee, sick may he be.
> May his strength depart!
> Do not thou remain by him,
> Come back, sound, to me.
> His strength lies here
> As the smoke blows away!

Leland goes on to say that to tell in which direction the stolen horse has been taken, you take a "sucking babe" to a stream and hold the child over the water, saying:

> Tell me, O Nivaseha,
> By the child's hand,
> Where is my horse?
> Pure is the child; pure as the sun,
> Pure as water, pure as the moon,
> Pure as the purest.
> Tell me, O Nivaseha,
> By the child's hand,
> Where is my horse?

To keep a horse from being stolen, when first acquired the animal is made to stand beside a small fire and then its back is brushed with a switch which has been half blackened with coal. As it is brushed, the owner will say the following spell.

Stay here, stay here!
Thou art mine.
Three chains I have,
I bind thee.
One is the land,
One is myself,
And one is God.

With a piece of coal or charcoal, a circle is then drawn on the left front hoof and a cross on the right front hoof. Then the Gypsy says:

Round, round and round!
Be thou, be thou very sound.
The devil shall not come to thee!
God shall be with thee.
Drive away from the horse's body
The Father of Evil!
Go not to any other man.
Be beautiful, frolicsome and good.
Seven spirits of earth hear!
I have seven chains.
Protect this animal ever, ever!

Then a piece of salted bread is fed to the horse, and the owner spits seven times across its face.

The Kukuya tribe of Hungarian Gypsies also places the horse beside a campfire. They dig a small hole in front of the horse and fill it with some straw and some hair from the horse's mane and tail. The animal's left front hoof is then scraped across the ground and dirt taken out of it and put into the hole. The Gypsy says:

A straw! A hair!
May you never be hungry.
May he who steals you die!
Like the hair and the straw,
May he go to the ground!
Earth, these things to thee.
May a sound horse be mine!

To keep a horse lively and in good spirits—especially just before a horse fair!—it is common practice to rub along its spine with garlic.

Where "man's best friend" is considered to be the dog, the Gypsy's best friend is his horse. However, almost every Gypsy family will have a dog (the Romany word for dog is *jukel*). They are a crossbreed known as "lurchers," usually having a lot of greyhound in them, along with strains of Scottish deerhound, wolfhound, collie, Alsatian, Bedlington or even Doberman. They are primarily hunting dogs, working with the Rom to hunt game of all sorts: pheasants, hares, rabbits, even hedgehogs. Where the horse is acceptable in Romany society—a Gypsy wouldn't think twice about drinking water where a horse had drunk—the dog is *mokkadi*, or "unclean," as is a cat, because dogs and cats clean themselves by licking their fur.

A shuvano in Scotland told of a love spell that he said was "infallible." You throw a cloth over two dogs that are mating. Then the cloth is given to the one you desire, with the words that follow.

The Gypsy's best friend.

I the dog, she the bitch,
(or "He the dog, I the bitch")
I the helve, she the axe,
I the cock, she the hen,
That, that I desire.

Many women, having received a cloth in this fashion and knowing the charm behind it, have made the cloth into a pillowcase or similar item, so that it will always be around, keeping the two of them together.

If a dog rolls on the ground at the foot of the steps up to the vardo, then he is watched closely. It is believed that a stranger will be coming from whichever direction the dog points when he stops rolling and stands up.

The cat (*matchiko*) is not seen a lot with Gypsy families. It is certainly not unknown, and you will sometimes see Gypsy children playing with a kitten, but it is not a common animal with the nomads. Perhaps this is because everyone and everything does its share of work in Gypsy life. Adults work, children work, horses work, dogs work, but you seldom see a cat working!

It is said that if a cat sits with its tail toward the fire, there is a cold spell coming. To carry a stray cat into the vardo is very bad luck, and Gypsy children are warned on no account to do this. Some Rom subscribe to the old belief that a cat will sit on the chest of a sleeping newborn child and "suck the breath" out of the child! Cats are therefore kept well away from all very young children.

Blackbirds, crows, rooks, and ravens are regarded favorably by the Rom. The raven, especially, is considered a very fortunate bird. Magpies are seen as warnings of problems to come. Owls are unfortunate birds. Large numbers of robins, if seen in the first week of December, indicate an early and hard winter.

Snakes are generally looked upon as lucky by the Rom. As mentioned in Chapter 6, a snakeskin is used to help cure rheumatism and stiffness of joints. Hungarian and Roumanian Gypsies will often camp for the winter in caves, high up in mountains. Powder made from dried snakes and lizards, found in the caves, is believed to have great magical properties. For instance, sprinkled on the marriage bed, it will bring long life and great happiness to the bride and groom.

On Iona and the other northern islands of Scotland, on Michaelmas Day (September 29), a large number of Gypsies would gather to race horses. Traditionally they would not ride their own horses. They would steal a neighbor's horse and ride it, bareback, and with a wife or girlfriend sitting astride the horse behind them. On Iona there is a circle of stones known as the "Hill of Angels." The Gypsies would race their horses around this stone circle. Afterward, they would feast on special cakes cooked by the women, known as "Michael cakes." On the Isle of Canna, they would all assemble at the graveyard, again riding bareback with a woman behind them. In this case the woman could not be the rider's own wife, but could be a neighbor's wife. They would then ride in procession from the graveyard to an old stone menhir. They would gallop three times, clockwise, around the menhir, then canter to the village inn for refreshments that featured a huge, round cake. All of this was supposed to ensure good luck and fertility for the tribe for the following year.

Up until very recent times, for a bridal party to meet a man on horseback as they made their way to the church was considered to be a sign of great luck. In the magazine *North-East Corner of Scotland,* in 1886, an article stated: "The meeting of a horse by a bridal party as the 'first fit' (animal or person first encountered) was looked upon as a sure proof of a happy marriage." Many a Gypsy would ride his horse where he knew there would be a wedding party, knowing they would give him a piece of silver in gratitude.

Many times, when a favorite horse dies, the owner will hang up the hooves in his vardo, as sacred objects, to keep away bad luck. To carry a horse's tooth in your pocket, or putsi, is to carry wealth and prosperity with you, say the Gypsies of the West Country of England.

If an unmarried woman finds a cast-off horseshoe, she should count the number of holes that are empty of nails. These represent the number of years before she will marry.

As the all-important source of power, the horse must be protected. For countless centuries this has been done by many cultures, not only Gypsies, with what have come to be known as "horse brasses." These have been found on all the great work horses: the Shires, the Clydesdales, the Suffolk Punches, the Cleveland Bays, the Hackneys, and so on. A horse brass is a symbol, or set of symbols, made out of brass and hung from the horse's harness. Sometimes a number of these brasses are hung together, mounted on a strip of leather known as a martingale. Dozens of symbols are used. Some of the oldest and most popular are the sun, the moon, stars, heart, cross, the triskele or three-legged sun-wheel. Geometric designs are used, bells, horses, acorns—just about anything that has meaning to the maker.

The brasses were originally worn to protect the horses from disease and from the evil eye. They were also worn to give strength and endurance, and to promote fertility. The most popular images remain the sun and the moon, in various representations. Sometimes there would be multiple moons, three crescents, or a crescent with a star inside it.

Many of the designs with a heart as the base were actually intended to "give heart" to the animal, to give it strength. Some Gypsies will wear these brasses themselves to promote love. It is not uncommon to see a horse brass hanging from a Romany woman's belt, or as a man's belt buckle. They can be heavy, but effective.

Horse Brasses.

15

TOOLS OF THE TRADE:
Aids and Extensions of Power

I nsofar as Gypsies generally use whatever is handy as tools for their magic, there really are no set implements for Gypsy witchcraft and magic. However, there are some items that are common among shuvanis and shuvanos.

The Putsi

The putsi is probably the most common magical item found among all Gypsies. This is a bag that varies in size; it can be as small as 1" x 2" or as large as 4" x 6"; it can have a drawstring top or a fold-over top. Most putsis are made out of fabric—pieces cut from old drapes, curtains, clothing, or even carpets. Some are made of leather. Most are decorated, usually by the addition of beads and/or buttons, or by embroidery. Many putsis are worn hanging from a cord around the neck; others hang from a belt.

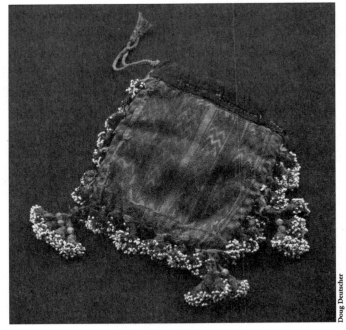

Putsi, or pouch. Roumanian, c. 1850.

148

The Kosh

Although "magic wands" are not often used as such, some shuvanis will utilize a wand-like piece of wood which they have lovingly cut, decorated, and polished—and in many instances have consecrated. This wand is usually about eighteen inches in length, and can be of hard or soft wood. Many, I found, were pieces of a branch cut from a tree that had been struck by lightning. This is thought to confer very powerful qualities to the wand.

The wand, or *kosh* (literally "stick"), is generally slightly tapered. Some have been stripped of bark; others are stripped except for about four inches at the base that serves as a handle. I've seen one or two with copper or even gold wire wound about them, in a spiral from tip to base. I have also seen one with a quartz crystal fastened to its tip, but the decoration—where there is any—is usually burned into the wood or painted on it. Various symbols are used. The choice of symbol(s) is the owner's.

To make the kosh sacred, it is consecrated by dipping it into a running stream. Various words are spoken. One chuvihano told me that he said:

> *Katar rook,*
> *Katar puv,*
> *Katar Mamus;*
> *Akai sor mi ruzlapen.*
>
> From the tree,
> From the earth,
> From the Mother;
> Here is all my strength.

Some koshes are cut with a forked end. They are used much like a Wiccan athame, as a projector of "power" (force, desire). When sending out a particular thought or spell, the shuvani will bring up the kosh dramatically, pointing it in the direction she is sending the thought.

The Gypsy's *kosh*,
or magic wand.

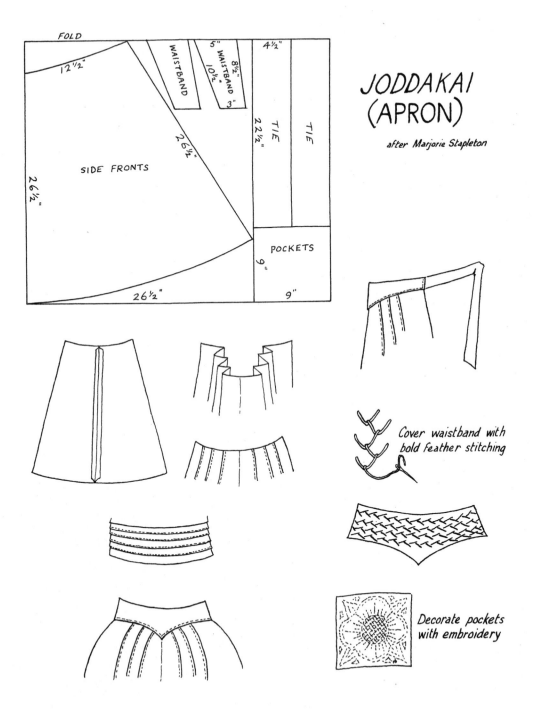

FOLD

12½"

WAISTBAND

5"
WAISTBAND
8½"
10½"
3"

4½"

SIDE FRONTS

26½"

26½"

TIE
22½"

TIE

POCKETS
9"

26½"

9"

JODDAKAI
(APRON)

after Marjorie Stapleton

Cover waistband with
bold feather stitching

Decorate pockets
with embroidery

Directions for making a *Joddakai*.

The Joddakai

Many Gypsy women will wear an apron, a *joddakai*. Most shuvanis also wear one, but they do so almost as though they were wearing a magical robe. The shuvani's apron is of a solid color—forest green, brown, dark blue, deep orange—with the waistband and pockets in a contrasting color. The pockets are large and seem to hold everything ever needed! On the previous page is a pattern for a typical one.

The Choori

The Romanes word for "knife" is *choori*. There is no special knife used, in the sense of a Wiccan athame, but just about every Rom and every shu-vano carries a choori. The "peg-knife," as it is sometimes called, is usually made from an old kitchen knife. The blade is pulled from the handle and a new handle made from wood, carved to comfortably fit the owner's hand. The blade is ground down until it is about three to four inches in length.

In the case of the shuvanos, the handle of the knife is often decorated. Again, the symbols used are those chosen by the individual for his or her own personal reasons.

A *choori*, used for carving.

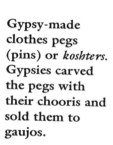

Gypsy-made clothes pegs (pins) or *koshters*. Gypsies carved the pegs with their chooris and sold them to gaujos.

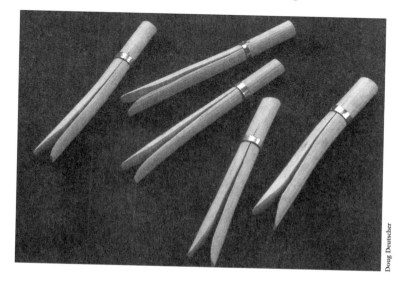

Doug Deutscher

A Gypsy's choori is kept razor sharp and used for every imaginable task. It is especially useful for carving clothespins and for making wooden chrysanthemums—a Gypsy specialty that is sold from door to door. For such wood carving, incidentally, the knife is held solidly against the Gypsy's knee and the wood is pulled against the blade.

The Bender Tent

The *bender* tent serves the shuvani much as a tepee or a wigwam might serve the Amerindian medicine man or woman. It is a place in which energy may be raised and concentrated. It is also a shelter from the elements and, duly consecrated, from outside forces of a more metaphysical nature. It might be used by the shuvani for the equivalent of a vision quest, or simply as a solitary place for the working of Gypsy witchcraft and magic. Often, when there is some special magic to be done, the shuvani will depart from the caravan and set up a bender in a clearing in a woods for several days, later to go back and rejoin the vardos.

To build a small bender is not difficult, as you can see here.

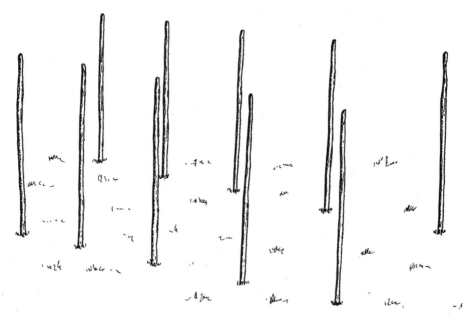

To make a bender tent, cut a dozen lengths of supple tree branches about ten feet long—hazelnut is preferred, but other wood will do. The ends of ten of the branches are stuck into the ground in two rows of five, at two-foot intervals as shown.

For the ridge pole, take a length of 2"x 4", about eight feet in length, and drill four sets of double holes at intervals along its length, as shown above.

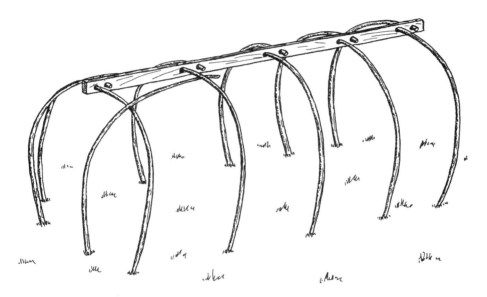

The tops of these side poles are then pushed into the ridge pole. The other two long poles are placed at one end (what will be the closed end of the bender) and bent over and lodged through the first two side poles.

This is your basic framework. Now throw tarps or even old blankets over this framework to cover it. To join the blankets, and to fasten them to the end poles, slits are cut in them and pieces of wood pushed through as shown here.

It can be seen that the finished size can vary, depending on the lengths of the poles used. A flap for closing the front can easily be incorporated if desired. Here is your magical bender, a suitable base for doing shuvani magic.

If a shuvani is working in her bender at the regular atchin' tan, or campground, and does not wish to be disturbed, then she will hang a blue cloth over the entrance to her bender to keep others away.

Dukkering with a Breadboard

In *Secrets of Gypsy Fortunetelling* (1988) I described a method of dukkering, or fortunetelling, spinning an ordinary kitchen knife on breadboard. As I said in that book: "A regular kitchen knife is used. It is placed in the center of the board. Around the edges of the board are placed pieces of paper...on which have been written suitable 'answers.'" Some of the most commonly used ones are:

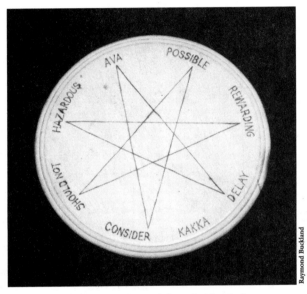

Breadboard used for *dukkerin'*.

Raymond Buckland

Yes
No
You must have patience
Beware of false friends
Good news is coming
A letter is expected
Success in business
An unexpected visitor
Love is here
Tears will turn to joy
News from abroad
A new admirer
An unexpected meeting
A journey
An important letter

The question is concentrated upon, then the querent spins the knife by its center. It is twirled three times in all, giving three messages. Of these, one (though not necessarily the first received) will be an answer to the original question, while the other two will be further messages which may or may not relate to it.

Although this form of fortunetelling is used by many Rom— even children will do it—it is also a form used by shuvanis. The difference is that while the "ordinary" travelers use an old kitchen breadboard, the shuvani will use a board kept especially for that divination. It may have started out as a breadboard but it is now kept carefully wrapped in cloth. Rather than laying out the "answers" on pieces of paper around the edge of the board, they have been permanently carved or burned into the wood.

The *yag*, the fire, is the focal point of the campsite. Here is a delightful Gypsy folk tale, about the coming of fire to the Gypsies, which was told to me by my grandfather.

THE QUEST FOR FIRE

There was a time when the gods felt that fire was too dangerous to be used by humankind. In those days the Rom would *jal a drom* (travel the road) gladly through the summer, but cold and miserable were the winters.

One fine day, a tribe sat on some rocks about their atchin' tan, enjoying the warm day. The puridai gazed up at the sun and said, "If only we had a piece of that, we could be warm all through the year."

Then young Bokka spoke up. He was the youngest son of the wagon wheel maker. "I will go and ask the gods for a piece of the sun," he said.

His older prals (brothers) laughed at him, but puridai nodded gravely. "It would be good," she said.

Bokka took some of his mother's good, unbaked bread and set off on his journey. His travels took him over hill and dale, across rivers and streams, through woods and across fields. One day he was passing an old barn, at the corner of a farmer's field, when he heard a small voice call out.

"Good sir, please help me!"

Bokka stopped and looked into the barn. The building was used for storing corn and nuts and was three-quarters filled with them, but in the front, near the door, sat several very large traps. In one of these traps, held fast, lay a large, black rat.

"Did you call out to me?" Bokka asked.

The rat nodded. "I am caught in the farmer's trap," he said. "You are a Romany; you know what it's like to be free. How would you like to be caught in a trap?"

"I wouldn't," said the young man. "But then I wouldn't get caught in the first place." He looked at the huge pile of grain and nuts. "Were you taking the farmer's grain?" he asked.

"There is plenty there for all," the rat replied. "Grain is free. The gods give it to us. The farmer should not begrudge me my small portion."

"I agree," Bokka said, and quickly he knelt and opened the trap. The rat ran out.

"I thank you, kind Rom," said the creature. "My name is Yag. I am forever in your debt. Let me ride with you, on your shoulder, so that I may help you in any way I can along the way."

Bokka placed the rat on his shoulder and off they went. As he walked, Bokka explained his mission, to find the gods and ask for a piece of the sun. Yag vowed that he would help.

After much journeying, late one evening, Bokka spied the atchin' tan of the gods. Their bright, colorful vardos were drawn up in a circle in the middle of a large clearing in the woods. All of the gods sat around, eating and drinking, laughing and singing. And there, in the middle of the circle, Bokka saw a piece of the sun. It lay on the ground, throwing out its light and its heat. The gods had placed a pot filled with bubbling water over it and had several *sushis* (rabbits) and *hotchiwitchis* (hedgehogs) on long skewers, slowly cooking by its heat. Bokka's mouth watered at the smells and, even from the edge of the trees, he could feel the warmth coming from the piece of the sun.

"I must ask the gods to let me have some sun to take home to my tribe," he said.

Yag laughed. "They will not give any to you."

"But the sun is like the corn and the grain, the nuts and the fruits of the trees," Bokka said. "It is there for everyone."

"Then how is it you don't already have a piece of the sun?" Yag asked.

Bokka couldn't answer.

"Well," said the rat, looking at the unhappy young Gypsy, "I guess it wouldn't hurt to ask."

Bokka eagerly got to his feet and went forward into the ring of light. The gods looked up in surprise to see him approach.

"Greetings, Mighty Ones," said Bokka, bowing his head. "I come to ask for a piece of the sun, to take home to my tribe. They are cold and would dearly love to have its heat."

The old puridai of the gods, a wisened old woman many centuries old, spoke. "You may eat and drink with us," she said. "But you may not take anything away with you."

Bokka, who had eaten little throughout his journey, sat and ate. Yag climbed down off his shoulder and gnawed on some vegetable roots. The gods watched in silence. Eventually Bokka once more got to his feet. "You are certain I may not take some of the sun with me?" he asked, hopefully.

"We are certain," said the old woman.

As Bokka turned, sadly, to leave, Yag moved across to where a length of fennel stalk lay at the edge of the ashes. He grasped it in his teeth and ran off into the woods with it. The gods laughed. "Your young friend must indeed be hungry," they said. "Let him keep the fennel stalk."

As young Bokka trudged back into the woods, away from the gathering of the gods, he felt a tear fall upon his cheek. He had failed. He had set out so full of hopes but now they were shattered. He must return to the cries of derision he knew he would hear from his brothers.

Two Flat Carts, with Accommodation tops.

It took many days to get back home to his tribe, but eventually Bokka came into the ring of vardos and saw the old familiar faces of family and friends. He took a breath. Now was the time to speak up and admit his failure.

"Here! Give them this," said a small voice.

Bokka looked down and saw Yag at his feet. The rat still held the fennel stalk between his teeth.

"Give them that?" said Bokka. "But why?"

"Just do as I say," said Yag.

So Bokka took up the fennel stalk and moved forward to where his father and mother, his brothers, the puridai, and all the others awaited him.

"Here," he said, and held out the fennel stalk. As he did so, he noticed a small trail of gray-blue smoke curling up out of the end of it. Fennel, like the elder, has a soft, pith core inside its sturdier outer casing. This core smoldered with the fire of the sun.

There was much rejoicing as the smoldering fennel was blown upon and used to light straws and then wood. Soon a great pile of sun-fire was blazing in the Gypsy camp.

"How can I ever thank you?" Bokka asked of his furry friend.

"It was simply my return for what you did for me," said Yag.

But from that day to this, the Romany word for fire is *Yag*, named after the King of the Rats.

At midsummer, known as *Shanti*, a special fire is built by many Gypsy tribes. The night before—Midsummer's Eve—is spent in darkness, in remembrance of the days when there was no fire, with no warmth or comfort, or means of cooking. Everything is quiet and hushed. No singing, no revelry. Then, at first light the next morning, a fire is lit by the Gypsy King, the tribal leader. A young boy then takes a faggot from that fire and goes around, from vardo to vardo, lighting all the other family fires.

A huge breakfast is cooked, with steaming mugs of tea, and singing, dancing, and general celebration follow.

16

GYPSY SHAMANISM
Greater Depths of the Mysteries

It is no wonder that the Gypsy, living so close to nature, should be regarded by many as a shaman. Shamans are found universally: among the Lapps, Siberians, Australians, Africans, Amerindians, and other tribal groups. In a sense the shuvani is very much a shaman, yet there are certain Gypsies who are even more so. They generally do not move about with a tribe, but are solitary Rom, living alone.

The shaman believes that all elements have their source of power in the spirit world and therefore are imbued with spirits that can be contacted at any time they may be needed. All life forms are, in this way, interconnected in a giant web of life. In this day and age you might think of it as being similar to the interconnection of the World Wide Web of the computer world. The shaman can move back and forth between the two worlds—that of the spirit and the mundane world—deliberately, as needed.

The specialties of a shaman are healing, accessing new and/or lost knowledge, developing power, and prophesying. All of this knowledge he obtains by going on the shamanic journey.

The shamanic journey is the usual method of communicating with your spirit self for the purposes of gaining knowledge, since your spirit self is in direct connection with all other spirit forms. The shaman will journey by descending into the earth, in his or her imagination. He or she does this by entering the earth down a hole, or through a cave or similar opening.

To arrive at the state of mind necessary for this journey, shamans train using a rapid, rhythmic drum beat, which is referred to as the horse, or *grai* (in Romanes)—the spirit travel vehicle. The grai of the Romany shaman is frequently played on a tambourine. This is beaten in what is known as the *desh* beat—ten beats in a pattern of three; three; two; two.

It is possible to learn to make the shamanic journey, and thereby to gain knowledge, whether it be something that was lost or something new that is sought. To do this, lie comfortably on your back, in a quiet setting where you will not be disturbed. Have a low light, or even darkness. With your eyes closed, take a number of slow, deep breaths, quieting your body and ridding it of any aches and pains or any extraneous thoughts. Now concentrate on what it is that you wish to know. Form a question in your mind, if necessary. After a few moments of thinking hard on this, let it go and again relax and breathe deeply.

Now concentrate your thoughts on a cave, or a hole in the ground or in a tree trunk, that you have either actually seen or that you can vividly see or create in your mind. Concentrate on it and see it in all its detail. See yourself advancing toward it, drawing closer and closer. See it as a small animal might see it, as it prepares to enter the hole. Then *you* enter it. Go into the hole; feel and sense it in every way possible. Smell the earth, or the wood of the tree. Hear the water trickling down the rock wall of the cave. Feel it; sense it; experience it.

Go farther into the cave, or deeper down the hole. As you do so, do not be surprised if you are met by somebody or something. It might be a person; it might be an animal; it might be no more than a ball of light, or a strong "impression" of a presence. Whatever it is, accept it and go with it. If you feel too apprehensive, you can ask the presence to assume a different form, one you feel more comfortable with. Then go with it as it leads you deeper into the earth. As you journey, ask your guide the question that you have. You will be led to the answer.

The answer to your question may be found when you are led into a room, a library, a school, out into a field, or anywhere at all. You may find yourself presented with a lecture by someone, a play or musical performance that you must interpret, an ancient volume to go through. Whatever the form, you will receive the answer to your question. When you have it, you must return the same way you came, back to the entrance hole. Your guide may or may not return with you. Before you step back into this mundane realm, thank your guide for the knowledge obtained.

Relax, breathe deeply, open your eyes and wake up. Immediately write down what you have learned.

This technique was given to me by an old Gypsy shaman named Grey Boswell, whom I found living on the Norfolk Broads in England. His home was an ancient upturned boat under some trees on the bank of the Broads River. He emphasized that it takes time to attune to the method, but assured me that just about anyone can journey in this manner, if they put their mind to it. I find that it helps immeasurably to make a tape recording of a drum beating—about 210 to 220 beats per minute—and have that playing very softly in the background. As you journey through the underworld, you may find yourself going through tunnels, sometimes upward and sometimes downward. It may be steep or not. If you encounter obstacles, there is usually a way around them.

You may well encounter a "Power Animal," according to Grey. Indeed, this may be the one who appears and leads you. Your Power Animal is a special source of personal power, something you can draw on in any time of need. If you don't feel that the creature leading you is your Power Animal, then ask to be taken to meet your animal. The Rom call this their *Pral* or *Pen* (literally meaning "brother" or "sister").

One way to judge whether or not the creature you meet—or one that is brought to you—is truly your Power Animal is to question it. Have your guide lead you to a comfortable place and then ask for your Power Animal to be brought to you. When it appears, question it. Ask about its qualities, its thoughts and feelings. Listen to the answers you get. Let the image fade and return. See how strongly it comes back. You will know by how comfortable you feel with it which is your true Pral or Pen.

One of the symbols of the shaman is the tree—for, like the shaman, while based on the earth, it reaches up into the sky yet also thrusts down into the depths beneath the earth; it connects humankind and spirit. Around the tree stretch the spokes of the Wheel of the World. The Romanes word for tree is *rook* and the word for wheel is *boler*, so this symbolism is referred to as the Rook and Boler.

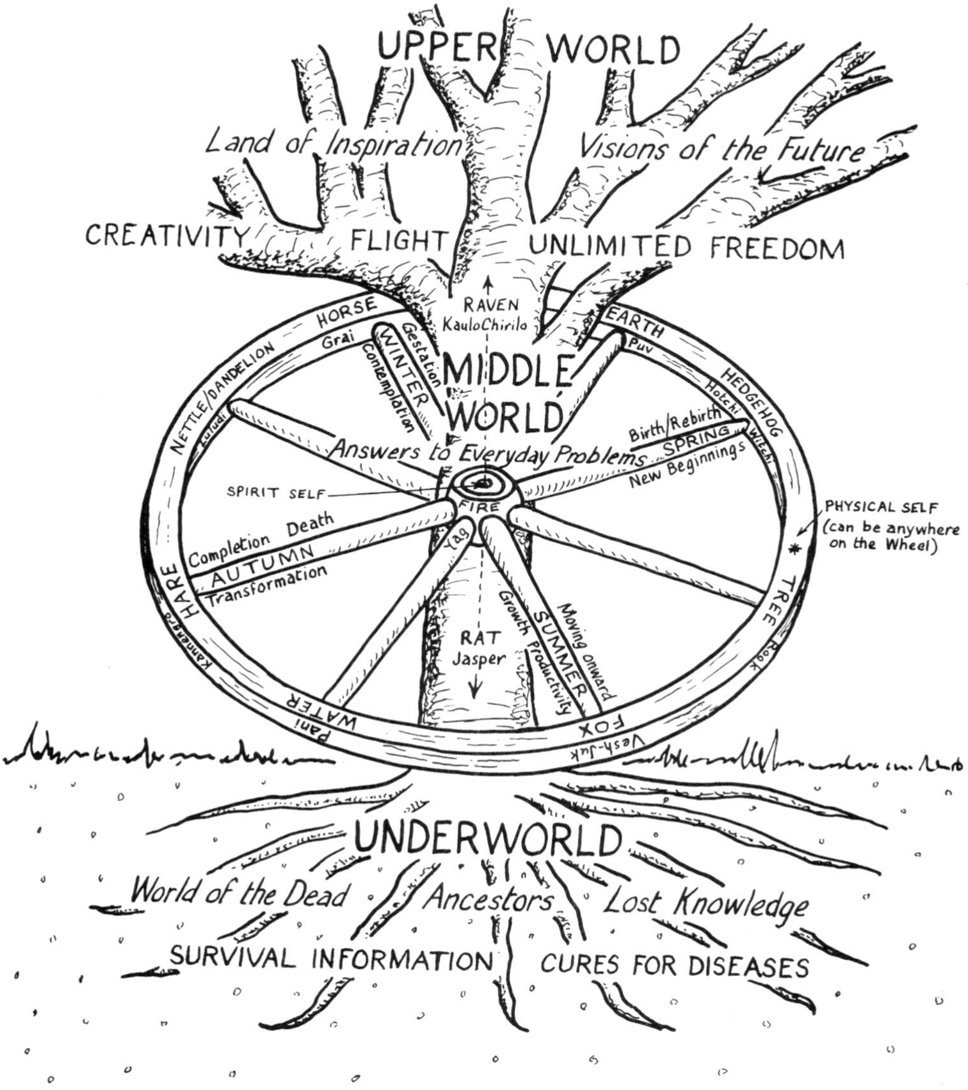
UPPER WORLD
Land of Inspiration
Visions of the Future
CREATIVITY
FLIGHT
UNLIMITED FREEDOM
RAVEN
KauloChirilo
HORSE
Grai
EARTH
Puv
NETTLE/DANDELION
Gestation
WINTER
Contemplation
MIDDLE WORLD
HEDGEHOG
Hotchi Witchi
Birth/Rebirth
SPRING
New Beginnings
Answers to Everyday Problems
SPIRIT SELF
FIRE
PHYSICAL SELF
(can be anywhere on the Wheel)
Completion Death
AUTUMN
Transformation
Yag
HARE
TREE
Rook
RAT
Jasper
Growth
SUMMER
Productivity
Moving onward
FOX
Vesh-Juk
WATER
Pani
UNDERWORLD
World of the Dead
Ancestors
Lost Knowledge
SURVIVAL INFORMATION
CURES FOR DISEASES

The Rook and Boler image combines the Shamanic Tree of Life and the Romany Medicine Wheel.

Study the Rook and Boler image and you can see how the Boler blends with the seasons of the year, and how its eight spokes are made up of those creatures and elements important to the Gypsy way of life. Shamanic journeying to the upper branches of the *Rook*, and to its deepest roots, can open you to life in its many aspects, and can answer for you some of life's greatest mysteries. It is your passport to Gypsy Witchcraft and Magic.

A Ledge Vardo and a Showman's Van—the old way of traveling contrasts with the new.

Romanes Word List

In recent years an attempt has been made to standardize Romanes, the English Gypsy language. Thomas Acton and Donald Kenrick, of Romanestan Publications, have produced a book titled *Romani Rokkeripen To-Divvus*—"Romany Language Today." This is a very commendable attempt to keep the English Romany speech alive. In their introduction to the book they say:

> Today…around half of the Traveling children of primary school age in England and Wales are being educated; the foundations of mass literacy are being laid. Many older primary and secondary school children want to use their own language in school, but do not know where to start. An abundance of written English is presented to them by way of example, but Romanes—well, how should it be written? How should it be spelled?….This book is aimed first of all at such young people.

Acton and Kenrick's book not only contains a Romanes–English/English–Romanes dictionary, but also goes into the grammar of Romanes and examines a number of texts.

On the following pages are a few Romany words, and their meanings, taken from this book and from other sources.

Numbers:

One: *Yek*	Seven: *Efta*
Two: *Dui*	Eight: *Teigh*
Three: *Trin*	Nine: *Enin*
Four: *Stor*	Ten: *Desh*
Five: *Panch*	Twenty: *Bush*
Six: *Shov*	Hundred: *Shel*

Above/Over: *Opré*

Airplane: *Sasterchirilo* ("iron bird")

Bird: *Chirilo*

Black: *Kaulo*

Blood: *Ratti*

Candle: *Mumeli*

Cat: *Matchiko*

Dance: *Khelapen*

Daughter/Girl: *Chavvi* or *Chai*

Death/Lifespan: *Meripen*

Doctor: *Drabengro* or *Mullomengro*

Dog: *Juk* or *Jukkel*

Ear: *Kan*

Earth: *Puv*

Feather: *Por*

Fire: *Yag*

Flower: *Luludi*

Fortunetelling: *Dukkering*

Fox: *Vesh-juk* ("woods dog")

Good Luck: *Kushti bok*

Half: *Posh*

Hare: *Kannengro* ("ear thing")

Hedgehog: *Hotchiwitchi*

Horse: *Grai*

Horseshoe: *Petalo*

Hot: *Tatti; Tatto*

I/Me: *Mandi*

Iron: *Saster*

Kettle: *Kavvi*

Kettle Iron: *Kavvi-saster*

Knife: *Chiv* or *choori*

Leaf/Sign: *Patrin*

Life: *Jivaben*

Locomotive: *Sastergrai* ("iron horse")

Month: *Shoon*

Name: *Nav*

Night: *Rarti*

Rabbit: *Sushi*

Rabbit Hole: *Beri*

Rat: *Jasper*

Ring: *Angushtri*

Salt: *Lon*

Silver: *Rup*

Smith/Farrier: *Petulengro*

Snake: *Sap*

Son/Boy: *Chavvo*

Spirit/Ghost: *Mullo*

Spirits/Whiskey: *Tatipani* ("hot water")

Stone: *Bar*

Summer: *Lilai*

Tambourine: *Baulo Tek* or *Tek*

Thank You: *Parika tut*

Tree: *Rook*

Unclean: *Mokkadi*

Wagon: *Waggon* or *Vardo*

Water: *Pani*

Wheel: *Boler*

Winter: *Ven*

Woods/Forest: *Vesh*

Writer: *Lavengro*

Year: *Bersh*

Yes; No: *Ava; Kakka*

You: *Tutti*

Young: *Tauni*

Youth: *Chal*

BIBLIOGRAPHY

Many books have been written about the Gypsies. However, the majority seem to be out of print. Copies have to be tracked down through book search companies, secondhand book stores, through inter-library loans, etc. Listed below are the books I have mentioned in the text, together with many others I think are well worth finding and reading. Some possible sources are: Cottage Books, Gelsmoor, Coleorton, Leicestershire LE67 8HQ, England; Graham York, 4 Bonds Cottages, High Street, Honiton, Devon EX14 8JU, England.

Acton, Thomas, and Donald Kenrick. *Romani Rokkeripen Todivvus*. London: Romanestan, 1984.

Adler, Marta. *My Life With the Gypsies*. London: Souvenir, 1960.

Algar, D. *Original Gypsy Remedies*. Essex: Algar, 1986.

Ayres, Edward. *Bender Tents*. London: Macmillan Education, 1979.

Bercovici, Konrad. *The Story of the Gypsies*. London: Jonathan Cape, 1929.

_____. *Gypsies, Their Life, Lore and Legends*. New York: Greenwich House, 1983.

_____. *Singing Winds: Stories of Gypsy Life*. New York: Greenwich House, 1926.

Borrow, George. *Lavengro*. London: Murray, 1851.

_____. *The Romany Rye*. London: Collins, 1857.

_____. *Romano Lavo Lil*. London: Murray, 1874.

Bowness, Charles. *Romany Magic*. York Beach, ME: Samuel Weiser, 1973.

Brown, Frances. *The Harefoot Legacy* (fiction). London: Headline, 1990.

_____. *Dancing On the Rainbow* (fiction). London: Headline, 1991.

_____. *The Other Sister* (fiction). London: Headline, 1992.

Buckland, Raymond. *Buckland's Complete Book of Witchcraft*. St. Paul: Llewellyn, 1986.

_____. *Secrets of Gypsy Fortunetelling*. St. Paul: Llewellyn, 1988.

_____. *Secrets of Gypsy Love Magic*. St. Paul: Llewellyn, 1990.

_____. *Secrets of Gypsy Dream Reading*. St. Paul: Llewellyn, 1990.

_____. *Buckland Gypsy Fortunetelling Deck*. St. Paul: Llewellyn, 1989.

_____. *Buckland Gypsies' Domino Divination Deck*. St. Paul: Llewellyn, 1995.

Cheiro. *Cheiro's Language of the Hand*. London: Nichols, 1897.

Clébert, Jean-Paul. *The Gypsies*. London: Penguin Books, 1967.

Croft-Cooke, Rupert. *A Few Gypsies*. London: Putnam, 1955.

Dearson, Seton. *The Gypsy Gentleman: A Study of George Borrow*. London: Murray, 1939.

Derlon, Pierre. *Secrets of the Gypsies.* New York: Ballantine, 1977.

Emerson, Alice B. *Ruth Fielding and the Gypsies* (fiction). New York: Cupples & Leon, 1915.

Evens, Bramwell. *Out With Romany: Adventures With Birds and Animals.* ULP, 1952.

_____. *Out With Romany Again.* ULP, 1938

_____. *Out With Romany, By Meadow and Stream.* ULP, 1942.

_____. *Out With Romany, By Moor and Dale.* ULP ,1944.

_____. *A Romany In the Fields.* London: Epworth, 1958.

Evens, Eunice. *Through the Years With Romany.* ULP, 1946.

Evens, G. Kinnaird. *Romany On the Farm.* London: Epworth, 1952.

Fonseca, Isabel. *Bury Me Standing.* New York: Knopf, 1995.

Fontana, Marjorie. *Cup of Fortune.* Wisconsin: Fontastic, 1979.

Fraser, Angus. *The Gypsies.* London: Blackwell, 1992.

Frater U∴D∴ *Secrets of Sex Magic.* St. Paul: Llewellyn Publications, 1995.

Goldberg, B. Z. *The Sacred Fire.* New York: University Books, 1958.

Golowin, Sergius. *The Gypsy Dream Book.* York Beach, ME: Samuel Weiser, 1987.

Grand Orient. *A Manual of Cartomancy.* London: Rider, 1912.

Greenfield, Howard. *Gypsies.* New York: Crown, 1977.

Gypsy Queen, A. *The Zingara Fortune Teller.* London: Street & Smith, 1901.

Hancock, Ian. *A Handbook of Vlax Romany.* Colombus, OH: Slavica, 1995

Hargrave, Catherine Perry. *A History of Playing Cards.* New York: Houghton Mifflin, 1930.

Harvey, Denis E. *The Gypsies: Waggon-Time and After*. London: Batsford, 1975.

Hornby, John. *Gypsies*. Edinburgh: Oliver & Boyd, 1965.

Jeffery, Juliet. *Gypsy Vans*. Chichester: Jeffery, 1983.

Jenkins, Herbert. *The Life of George Borrow*. London: Murray, 1924.

Jones, E. Alan. *Gypsy Caravans*. Yorkshire: Signs, 1981.

_____. *Yorkshire Gypsy Fairs, Customs & Caravans 1885–1985*. Yorkshire: Hutton, 1986.

Kenrick, Donald, and Sian Bakewell. *On the Verge: The Gypsies of England*. University of Hertfordshire Press, 1990.

King, Charles. *Men of the Road*. London: Muller, 1972.

Kohn, Bernice. *The Gypsies*. New York: Bobbs-Merrill, 1972.

Lee, Ronald. *Goddam Gypsy*. New York: Bobbs-Merrill, 1972.

Leland, Charles Godfrey. *The English Gypsies and Their Language*. London: Trubner, 1874.

_____. *Gypsy Sorcery & Fortune Telling*. London: Fisher-Unwin, 1891.

Lucas, Richard. *Common and Uncommon Uses of Herbs for Healthful Living*. New York: Arc Books, 1969.

Maas, Peter. *King of the Gypsies* (fiction). New York: Viking, 1974.

Maple, Eric. *The Dark World of Witches*. London: Robert Hale, 1962.

Marre, Jeremy, and Hannah Charlton. *Beats of the Heart*. London: Pluto, 1985.

Martin, Kat. *Gypsy Lord* (fiction). New York: St. Martins, 1992.

Martin, Kevin. *The Complete Gypsy Fortuneteller*. London: Arlington, 1973.

McDowell, Bart. *Gypsies: Wanderers of the World.* Washington D.C.: National Geographic Society, 1970.

McGaa, Ed (Eagle Man). *Mother Earth Spirituality: Native American Paths to Healing Ourselves & Our World.* San Francisco: HarperRow, 1990.

Minetta. *The Art of Tea-Cup Fortune Telling.* London: Foulsham, 1958.

North, Grace May. *Nan Of the Gypsies* (fiction). Saulfield, OH: Buccaneer Books, 1926.

Paulton's Romany Museum. *Romany Life and Customs.* Hampshire: Paultons, 1984.

Petulengro, Gypsy. *Romany Hints for Hikers.* London: Methuen, 1936.

———. *Romany Herbal Remedies.* Newcastle: Borgo Press, 1982.

Petulengro, Leon. *Romany Boy.* London: Hale, 1979.

Sandford, Jeremy. *Gypsies.* London: Abacus, 1975.

Sampson, John. *Gypsy Folk Tales.* New Hampshire: Salem House, 1984.

Smith, D. J. *Discovering Horse-Drawn Caravans.* Buckinghamshire: Legacy Books, 1981.

Smith, Martin Cruz. *Gypsy In Amber* (fiction). New York: Ballantine, 1971.

Soper, Irene. *The Romany Way.* Wiltshire: Ex Libris, 1994.

Stanley, Denise, and Rosy Burke. *The Romano Drom Song Book.* Oxford: Burke, 1971.

Stapleton, Marjorie. *Make Things Gypsies Made.* London: Studio Vista, 1976.

Stapley, L. and J. *Olde Way Crafts.* Cornwall: Stapley, 1993.

Thompson, John. *Making Model Gypsy Caravans*. Hampshire: Thompson, 1978.

_____. *Carts, Carriages & Caravans*. Hampshire: Thompson, 1980.

Tong, Diane. *Gypsy Folktales*. San Diego: Harcourt Brace Jovanovich, 1989.

Trigg, Elwood B. *Gypsy Demons and Divinities*. Seacaucus, NJ: Citadel, 1973.

Varney, Joyce. *The Half-Time Gypsy*. New York: Bobbs-Merrill, 1968.

Vesey-Fitzgerald, Brian. *Gypsies of Britain*. London: Chapman & Hall, 1944.

Vince, John. *Discovering Horse Brasses*. Buckinghamshire: Shire, 1968.

Von Hausen, Wanja. *Gypsy Folk Medicine*. New York: Sterling, 1992.

Ward-Jackson, C. H., and Denis E. Harvey. *The English Gypsy Caravan—Its Origins, Builders, Technology and Conservation*. Newton Abbot: Devon, David & Charles, 1973.

Williams-Ellis, Amabel. *Gypsy Folk Tales*. London: Pan Books, 1973.

Wood, Manfri Frederick. *In the Life of a Romany Gypsy*. London: Rowtledge & Kegan Paul, 1973.

Yates, Dora. *Gypsy Folk-Tales*. London: Phoenix House, 1948.

Index

GYPSY FORTUNE TELLING TAROT KIT
Raymond Buckland
(Formerly titled *Buckland's Complete Gypsy Fortuneteller*)

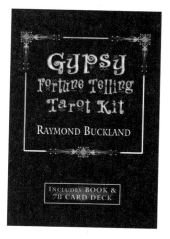

Look into your future through the mysterious art of Gypsy fortunetelling. Raymond Buckland, who is from an authentic Gypsy family, reveals the secrets of palmistry, crystal-gazing, card reading and divining the future through common household items. Includes the *Buckland Gypsy Fortunetelling Deck*, which are the actual cards created and used by the Buckland Gypsies themselves, along with the book *Gypsy Fortune Telling and Tarot Reading*. Amaze your friends and yourself as you use these cards to tap into your psychic powers. The *Gypsy Fortune Telling Kit* will bring you and your family hours of entertainment as well as enlightenment.

• Read palms, tea leaves, cards

• See the future using common household items: knives, dice, needles, stick

• Learn to interpret the weather and the actions of animals

Boxed set: 78 full-color Gypsy cards; 5 ³⁄₁₆ x 8, 240-pp. illus. book
1-56718-091-4   **$24.95**

SECRETS OF GYPSY LOVE MAGICK
Raymond Buckland, Ph.D.

One of the most compelling forms of magick— perhaps the most sought after—is love magick. It is a positive form of working, a way to true delight and pleasure. The Gypsies have long been known for the successful working of love magick.

In this book you will find magicks for those who are courting, who are newlyweds, and love magick for the family unit. There is also a section on Gypsy love potions, talismans and amulets.

Included are spells and charms to discover your future spouse, to make your lover your best friend and to bring love into a loveless marriage. You will learn traditional secrets gathered from English Gypsies that are presented here for the first time ever by a Gypsy of Romani blood.

0-87542-053-2, 176 pp., mass market, illus.   **$4.99**

THE BUCKLAND GYPSIES' DOMINO DIVINATON DECK
Raymond Buckland

Here's a new, easy, and fun way to divine the future! Dominoes have been a favorite game for generations—but the Gypsies also use dominoes for telling fortunes, or *dukkerin'*. The Buckland Gypsies of England developed the idea of marking the domino "dots" on a blank deck of cards, so they could be easily carried.

Here is an easy-to-interpret domino divination deck that can be laid out in various spreads to tell you your fortune, lucky numbers, and lucky days of the week. This deck of 28 color cards comes boxed with a booklet illustrating each card and describing how to do accurate domino readings for yourself and friends, using four domino card spreads. The booklet also explains how to use a modified form of numerology with the cards and how to play dominoes for fun. Try this unique system of Gypsy divination and learn all about your future!

1-56718-094-9, 32 pp. booklet, 28 full-color cards   **$12.95**

BUCKLAND'S COMPLETE BOOK OF WITCHCRAFT
Raymond Buckland

Here is the most complete resource to the study and practice of modern Wicca, a lavishly illustrated, self-study course for the solitary or group. Included are rituals; exercises for developing psychic talents; information on all major "sects" of the Craft; sections on tools, beliefs, dreams, meditations, divination, herbal lore, healing, ritual clothing and more. This book unites theory and practice into a comprehensive course designed to help you develop into a practicing Witch, one of the "Wise Ones." Ray Buckland is a famous and respected authority on Witchcraft. Large format with workbook-type exercises, profusely illustrated and full of music and chants. Takes you from A to Z in the study of Witchcraft.

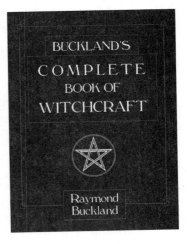

Traditionally, there are three degrees of advancement in most Wiccan traditions. When you complete studying this book, you will be the equivalent of a Third-Degree Witch. If you want to become a Witch, or if you merely want to find out what Witchcraft is really about, you will find no better book than this.

0-87542-050-8, 272 pp., 8 1/2 x 11, illus., softcover   **$14.95**